Being Brave Too

A novel and guide

Hester Leung and Sema Musson

Illustrated by Jelena Sinik

This one is for my Mum. Without her quiet courage,
Kaela and I would not have the life we have today.
And always for Kaela.

Hester

To my muses – Summer, lover of birds and
Stella, confident and courageous.

Sema

Reviews

Being Brave Too is a unique book about the story of friendship and having courage to stand in your own power. Told through the eyes of three girls with emails, letters and journal notes, the story canvasses a revived friendship, reconnections with a matriarch and dealing with bullying on social media.

I enjoyed how the entwined tips and skills equip young women to deal with life's challenges, especially through adolescence where the negative voice can get loud and unruly. But taking on a cause bigger than yourself is always a way to find your own resilience. Caring for the environment and wildlife can shine a light on the interconnectedness of life. The messages of strength and the tools to plan and deal with life are well integrated into the story, making it an interesting empowering read.

Dr Terri Janke, Indigenous leader, solicitor and CEO of Terri Janke and Company

If you are a parent wondering if you should give this book to your daughter (or son) then I recommend you do. *Being Brave Too* is full of the tales of girls growing up, experiencing so much in life. It reminded me of the first time my daughter, Katie, mentioned Best Friends Forever, having to wear the same thing as a best friend (or not!), school trips and birthday parties (lots of them), winning, losing, dreams and being scared, boys. So many things, hopes and expectations.

Being Brave Too shows the importance of being resilient and fearless or to fear less. It is also a reminder that the learning does not stop, growing continues, change happens, and that our daughters will get through it positively with the right tools and support.

David Turnbull, Leadership and executive coach and father to Katie

Contents

A note from Sema and Hester

At the time of writing this book we are in quite unusual times. It's like a parallel universe. We are all at home. We are working from home. Our daughters are being schooled from home. We have replaced our weekend catch-ups with virtual coffees and lots of phone calls and messages. The world is in a space of social distancing with the COVID-19 pandemic. It has been the most unusual year. COVID-19 in Australia has followed what has also been one of the most devastating bushfire seasons impacting our people, wildlife and the environment. It has required courage as we sit at home, and read and watch these sad events on our screens.

When we finished our first book, *Being Brave*, we were grateful for the number of girls who reached out to us to tell us how they could relate to the book. How it helped them deal with difficult relationships and situations at school. The media also started to talk to us about social media and bullying. So we wanted to expand on these themes in *Being Brave Too*.

As we sit at home in a world where social media is more important than ever for social connection and as we return to a new normal – one where we interact more online, where social media has an increased role for connecting with friends – we wanted to equip girls to manage the use of these tools positively.

More than ever we need to remain soft and strong. We need to remain kind to others and be confident that everything is going to be okay. We need to stop the negative self-talk, that little voice inside that tells us we can't do something or that we will fail if we try. This is our shadow-self. We hope *Being Brave Too* inspires a sense of hope and motivation. We are a tribe. We are all The Being Brave Girls.

Sema and Hester

Ellie Jones

June 7th

FunStar routines and gymnastics.

Burritos, drawing, dogs and daydreaming.

Long division and creepy crawlies.

AGE 13

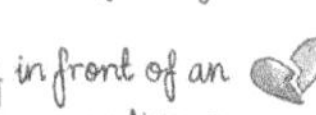

February 16th

Yoga, dancing and online games where you build cities.

Experiments, cooking and bubble egg waffles from Hong Kong.

Performing in front of an audience.

Alyssa Tan

AGE 12

Lucy Jones

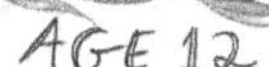

November 10th

Crab spotting, bird watching and swimming.

Mermaids and dragons.

Being bored.

AGE 7

Let's go

Alyssa

Thank goodness we're finally flying! We've been sitting on the runway for 53 minutes, 21 seconds exactly. Not that I've been looking at my watch every three minutes. I don't like being late.

I glance outside the window next to me. The houses look tiny from up here. Rows and rows of terracotta roofs form orangey-brown blobs. Like someone carelessly squeezed out the final bits of orangey-brown paint from a nearly empty tube. Splat! Then some green paint for the parks and gardens. Splodge! Then they used a paint brush to smear in roads, curving one way and joining into another. So irregular but hey, it seems to work. The city shrinks smaller and smaller and gives way to paddocks and fields. Patches of earthy brown dot the landscape where once they were probably green. On the horizon I can see the mountains, hazy and smoky.

We're higher now, above the ocean. A vast expanse of blue. Then it's just clouds. Us in the clouds. My grandma, or Por Por as I call her, used to tell me about a Chinese myth about dragons that breathe out clouds. In turn the clouds would produce rain, renewing life. She told me, "Clouds are dragons' breath. It's chi – the life-giving force." Where is that life now?

I stare into the sky for a while, lost in thought, thinking back over the year. My eyes well up with tears but I blink them away. I pull down the plastic blind, shutting out the clouds and the outside world and sigh. It's been a tricky time. No, it's been a tricky six months.

Dad turns to me from his seat. He looks at me intently but with kind eyes. "They're serving lunch now, Lyssie. I'm going to get the beef, but I'm guessing the chicken and rice for you?"

"Sure, that's fine. This plane smells." I shift in my seat uncomfortably and rub my eyes quickly to make sure Dad doesn't see the tears.

I bend down to grab my laptop out of my backpack. I'm one of the shortest in my year at school, but these seats are seriously tight. Dad's knees are touching the seat in front of him so I'm glad I don't have long legs.

I finally manage to wriggle out my laptop and place it on the tiny table in front of me. I open the mail folder. The latest email from Ellie way back in May is still there in my inbox – over six months ago now. I haven't deleted it yet.

Ellie is one of my best friends. Well, was… I haven't seen Ellie since her birthday party in June. I re-read her last email.

From: Ellie Jones
To: Alyssa Tan
Re: You're invited to my birthday party!!!
Sunday 24 May at 9:03am

Hey Lys, as you know it's my birthday in 2 weeks! Super excited – I'm going to be 13! Can you believe it? I'm having a sleepover on Saturday 6 June, the day before my birthday. Only 3 friends allowed. I've got my two besties from school, and you.

You haven't met Josie and Ruby yet. We've become really, really close this year. You will love them… I hope!

Josie plays the guitar and is really sweet and fun. Ruby has three dogs and has an ace voice, so we really get along. They live close by so they come over nearly every Saturday to hang. We do videos and make up dance routines, you know, the usual.

Anyway it would be great to see you again. I know it's been forever since we saw each other. Hope that robotics project went well. Okay, bye! Let me know if you can make it.

Love Ellie xx

It still hurts thinking back to that sleepover. I try not to go back to that day too much. Anyway, something even worse has happened since then that makes me being upset about Ellie's birthday party seem so pointless. Yet I can't shake the feeling from that day which is mixed up with all of the other sadness swirling around me.

In the last week of school, just two weeks ago, Por Por died. She used to live near us and looked after me ever since I was little. She's been a big part of my life. Earlier in the year she decided to go back to Hong Kong, where she was born. She missed her family who still lives there and she hadn't seen them for ages. She decided to go and live with her sister, my Great-Aunt Lily, in Hong Kong for a while.

I like to remember her when we waved goodbye in March at this very airport that we just flew out from. Mum and I stood there waving furiously at the departure gate.

We called out, "Bye, don't forget it's Gate 36! Ask someone if you need help. Gate 36!"

She was carrying her usual huge black leather handbag, wearing her usual old faded jeans, slip-on sneakers, with a crazy coloured knitted top. She used to knit or crochet all the time – tops, jumpers, blankets. There were so many things. She would donate the blankets to a homeless shelter and give out tops or jumpers to random people. Mostly she would wear her own designs. I still remember the top she had on – it was blue with red hearts. I loved that top. She was 70 years old and would wear these super loud jumpers!

She fell sick though, a few months into her visit. It got so bad, Mum flew to Hong Kong too. At first we thought she could come back with Mum and get better here, but Por Por didn't want to leave. After Mum made a couple of trips there and back, the doctor told Mum that Por Por wasn't going to get better. Mum arranged to work from Hong Kong and she's been living there since the end of September. I've been living with Dad.

Dad's been great. Of course, I stay with him every other weekend and holidays anyway. We have our own rhythm. But I miss Mum. How she sometimes fluffs my cheeks with her makeup brush, how she asks me which skirt to wear to work, how she makes pancakes. And Por Por… I don't even want to think about all the things. I can't…

Dad and I are flying to Hong Kong now for Por Por's memorial service. It's the start of summer holidays now, so we're going to stay in Hong Kong for the whole of December. I've never been there before. Mum, Dad and I will come back home together in the new year.

I haven't told Ellie any of this. My other best friends from school know what's going on, but Ellie, she's my oldest friend. It feels weird that Ellie doesn't know this massive part of my life. Up until June, I'd tell her everything.

Ellie and I became friends in preschool, but we changed schools in Year 6. She moved houses and I got into a private school. But we kept seeing each other heaps. We played soccer together and we would email or call. I stopped soccer at the start of this year because I didn't get into the mixed All Star Team our club was putting together. I put my name down but didn't get called to try out for it. Maybe Coach already knew he didn't want me.

With all the changes last year, Ellie fell into a slump. She was worried about making new friends, her little sister Lucy was bugging her and her parents were stressed about work and money. One day after soccer, we went to the library and read a story about a mythical Ayrebird who brings good luck to whoever sees it! We thought if we saw one, maybe Ellie would feel better. We shared an amazing, magical adventure but it feels so long ago now.

When I stopped soccer, I stopped seeing so much of Ellie. Then we had that fight. Since we're no longer speaking, I haven't had the courage to email Ellie either, to tell her what's happened. It's been so long that it would be weird to email her now. She's probably too wrapped up doing her own thing to have time to wonder about what's going on with me anyway.

This past year Ellie is always with her other friends, posting on her FunStar account, hanging out at the shopping centre. She's a great singer and confident in front of the camera. She does these clips and posts them on FunStar, an app where you put up videos. Mostly people sing or dance, but sometimes they talk about things that interest them too. I don't have an account but my cousin Max, who also knows Ellie, keeps showing them to me. She's great in them – confident in a way I don't know how to be. It's in the way she carries herself. Me, my eyes get all shifty on camera and I look away too much! Urghhh, I love dancing but I'm so awkward when I know I'm on camera.

In the past year, Ellie and I have become very different and grown apart. We're each hanging out with our own groups from school. Maybe that's the way things are going to be now.

Dad turns to me and gestures at the flight attendant holding a tray of food. I close my laptop and drop it back into my backpack. As Dad places the tray onto the little table, I grab the headphones and scroll through the movies. Anything to stop my mind churning.

FunStar

Ellie

I add in some sparkles to the top of the clip, choose my usual "strawberry pop" filter, then click "post." So cool! I love posting on FunStar. It's my escape – I love to find a song that matches how I feel, make up the routine, decide how the clip should look, then post it. I like seeing the love heart icon next to my username (ElsBels13) fill up with colour as more and more people watch what I've posted. Good to see all those people appreciate what I do!

I get it. I shouldn't like it. But it's a thrill anyway, and besides I did check with Mum that I can have the account, and Mum follows me too – so she knows what I'm doing. I always follow her rules. I only post once a week on the weekends and plan the posts after I've done my homework. There's still a few weeks until school goes back, so I can plan out a few more posts these holidays.

Suddenly Lucy barges into my bedroom. "Elliieeee!" she yells. "Where's my koala hairbrush? You've taken it again. Mum said you can't use it."

I glare at her. "Knock. You have to knock!" I raise my voice as I move to shove her out of my room. "Why is there no privacy in this house? Go away. You have to knock first!"

"But you took my stuff. That stops Rule #4. The Knock First Rule. If you take someone's stuff then you've also broken a rule. That means all other rules can be broken to fix the first broken rule. Gosh, you're dumb. How can you not know that?"

"Mum!" I yell, frustrated. "Lucy just stormed into my room without knocking. She's insulting me and without any evidence, claims that I took her koala hairbrush. Why would I take her stupid koala hairbrush? I'm not seven years old. I have my own hairbrush. Why would I use a koala shaped hairbrush, anyway? I'm not a baby." I say that last word directly at Lucy.

Mum comes down the hall. She's exasperated but not angry yet. "Okay, girls, what's happening? Who took what when where now…?"

Lucy and I both speak at once. A rabble of words. Quick and fast.

"She took it. I know she did. She –"

"No, I didn't. Search my room if you like."

"It's my favourite –"

"This is so stupid. I have no idea –"

" – and I saw you used it in your post!"

" – OMG, that was so last week. I put it back on your shelf and you let me."

"Well, it's not there anymore!"

"Clearly it's because you lost it. Don't blame me for your stupidness."

"That's not even a word."

"It is. As if you would know."

"Okay, girls," Mum steps in. She physically stands between us and separates us with outstretched arms. "Lucy, go into your room and cool down. When did you use your hairbrush last? We'll look for it now. And you, Ellie, if I find out you did take it for your video without asking, you will be banned from using that app. There are rules and consequences. You are getting too addicted to that thing."

I think about snapping back that I have been following her rules, but think better of it. It's not fair. Lucy always gets her way. I open up FunStar and scroll through my feed to take my mind off my annoying sister. Here's the one from my birthday! We're in the backyard. There's Josie and Ruby in matching dresses singing Happy Birthday! They look so good together, swaying to the music. The video switches to me moving in between them. Then we sing *Girls We Rule the World*! We had so much fun doing that video. It's perfectly choreographed. We are in time, it looks great!

There's a wisp of black hair at the patio door barely visible in the background. Was that Lys watching us? I stop the video, rewind, zoom in and play it again. I do that a few times. It's not super clear as she's blurred out in the background, but I'm sure now it's Lys. She has smooth hair that flows. Would look so great in a video doing a ponytail spin. If she'd only let me film her!

That afternoon she told me she was going to help Lucy with her science project, so I could go ahead and do the *Girls We Rule the World* dance clip with the others. She didn't want to be in it. She said she was self-conscious with these things.

I flop onto my bed and close the app on my phone. I stare at my bag hanging behind my door and take a deep breath. I think back to the night of my sleepover birthday party. Lys and I had a big fight. To be honest, I didn't want to invite Lys. One time she said FunStar was silly and made fun of this girl's dance routine… okay, I laughed at that girl's dance routine too. But it made me feel dumb next to her. Besides she doesn't know Josie and Ruby, who I met because they're into FunStar too. We became friends through an after-school group that teaches you dance routines and different ways to film and use the app.

I knew she wouldn't get along with Josie and Ruby as all we talk about is FunStar, singing and making up new routines. Mum was the one who wanted me to invite Lys, even though I explained to her I'd rather do something with Lys separately.

Lys is super smart and already knows she wants to do something sciency when she grows up. She's so lucky she's good at school stuff. She used to help me with my maths homework and she can do all the sums quickly in her head. Last year I was really down on myself for not being good at maths but now I know what my strengths are – I like being creative. This is why I love FunStar so much. It makes me happy that people encourage me to do what I'm good at and I've made great friends through it.

Lys just doesn't understand. That night Lys was hanging out with Lucy and I overheard her in Lucy's room, saying, "What's with that app obsession? It's a little lame, isn't it?"

I peeped into Lucy's room. Lucy was singing into her koala hairbrush and they were both laughing and dancing to *Girls We Rule the World*. As I watched Lys move, I remembered she's a good dancer. It was a much better routine than mine.

I couldn't help it. I stormed in and yelled, "Well, I love it. It makes me happy. Lys, you used to dance with me! What's your problem?"

Lys stopped dancing immediately. She dropped her hands by her side. She was quiet at first, glaring at me. Then she said, "You've always got these other people around you all the time. I don't fit in. You make me feel horrible."

"Well, I can't help it if you don't like it…" I say.

"You've changed," says Lys.

"What's wrong with you? I haven't… No, maybe I have. And for the better. I don't want to speak to you anymore," I said, and left Lys with Lucy.

In the morning, Lys was gone. Her mum must have picked her up before we woke up. Just like her to go running to her mum.

Maybe we're different now. I read somewhere friends come and go and you have to let the ones who hold you back go. I have all my other friends now and my FunStar followers. I pick up my phone and message Josie and Ruby to see what they're up to.

Bad hair day

Lucy

After Mum helps me find my koala hairbrush, I feel awful. Okay, so it fell into the laundry basket in the bathroom. My bad, but I know Ellie uses it without asking. I pick out a wavy blonde hair from the hairbrush and toss it onto the carpet in my bedroom. My hair is darker and straighter. It's in between Ellie's and Lys's hair.

Sometimes I feel like that. In between. Not wavy and soft pretty blonde, not straight glossy black. It's so boring. I'm so bored. I want my hair to be pink and blue. I want it to be like a mermaid. I want to be a mermaid! That would be awesome! I wonder how I make my hair pink and blue? There's that stuff Mum puts into the cupcake frosting. The red colouring that turns the frosting pink.

I wander into the kitchen. Where does Mum put the cake-making things? Oh yeah, in that box with all the colourful patty pans. Haha – pink hair! It will look so great.

I find the bottle of pink stuff. I untwist the lid and give it a sniff. I squeeze a couple of drops onto my fingers. It's a bit globby and looks really red. But I've seen Mum use it on cupcakes so it must work. I'll give it a go! I tip the bottle all over the top of my head, give it a big squeeze and can feel the cold gel plop on my head. I smear it around.

I can't see what I've done so I run into the bathroom to take a look in the mirror. Nope, nothing yet. My hair's a bit darker on the bit with the colour goop. I turn on the tap, wet my hands and put water on the colour goop on the top of my head. I add lots more water.

Okay – something's happening! I rub the pink water into my hair and it looks nice and wet. It's starting to look pinkish! Yay! I grab my toothbrush and start brushing it through. Oops, there's too much water now. It runs down my head onto my forehead, into my eyes and down my neck. The pink starts staining my t-shirt. Gosh, my hands are even pink! I turn the tap even more and grab the soap to wash my hands. As I'm trying to wipe the water out of my eyes with the back of my hands, I realise I've turned the tap up way too far and the bottle of food colouring which I left in the sink is turning everything pink. Pink sudsy water splashes everywhere! The sink, the counter-top, the floor... oh no, Mum is going to get seriously mad! Even the gaps between the tiles are going pink.

I grab a towel and try cleaning up. I turn off the tap with my pink soapy hands. The towel's got pink handprints all over it, like the tea towels you get from preschool with all the kids' handprints, but uglier. Way uglier. I start to panic. I look at myself in the mirror and realise my hair is sopping wet and there's also a pink collar stain around my t-shirt. Not good.

I open the cabinet under the sink to see what's in there that I can use to clean up and fix the towel. I see a box of the stuff Mum puts in her hair to get rid of "her greys." Maybe that'll get rid of "the pinks"?

I open the box and take a look at the instructions. Hmmm, big words I can't read. Maybe I should call Ellie now to help me. Nah, she'll just tell Mum. Better to fix it on my own.

I grab the box and squeeze the tube into the little bowl that comes inside the box, and mix it up with some other liquid stuff from the bottle. Just like I see Mum do. It smells and I scrunch up my nose. I use my toothbrush to paint the pasty white stuff onto the pink handprints on the towel. I take off my t-shirt and do the same on the collar. Then I look at my hair with globs of red goop on it. It hasn't turned really pink yet. Maybe if I use the stuff in the box my hair will look like Mum's after this. Blonde like Ellie's. So I use my toothbrush and smear some white paste onto my hair too mixing it in with pink. There's a little cute shower cap in the box, which I put on my head. I look like a chef!

In the meantime, I clean up the pink water on the floor and put the towel into the laundry basket together with my t-shirt. I reckon once Mum washes them, they'll be as good as new! I survey the bathroom and it looks pretty clean now. Good job, Lucy! The last step on the back of the box has a cartoon lady washing her hair. So I step into the shower to wash mine. Mum will be so pleased I'm taking a shower today without her telling me!

After a good shampoo, I step out of the shower. Urgh, my hands are still bright pink! I wipe away the fog on the mirror with my bright pink hands and take a look at myself. I stare at my reflection. In particular, I look at my hair. Wow, my hair has turned PINK. And I love it!

My moment of happiness runs down the drain as Mum opens the door.

"LUCYYYYYYYY! What have you done? Go to your room!"

To anyone who will lissen,

Mum hates my hair. I'm stuck in my room.

I have nothing to do than rite this stupid letter.
So borinnnggggg.

Ellie gets away with anything. Getting dresed up
and sneeking Mum's makeup for FunStar. all I did
was put some colour in my hair and its awesome.
And its making my pillow pink.

Saddness (but pink)

Lucy

Feeling grateful

Alyssa

The carnations smell of nothing. They have no smell. I wish they would smell like Por Por – soft, powdery, warm and cosy. I give them another sniff but still nothing.

I'm standing with Mum at the memorial service in a function centre where all of Mum and Por Por's relatives are gathered. We're at the door, smiling politely at people as they come in to speak to Mum and Great-Aunt Lily.

Mum looks tired. She's wearing a black dress which I don't recognise and her eye make-up is smudged. Her eye make-up is always smudged a little, but today it looks extra smudged as she wipes her eyes again with a crumpled tissue. She's speaking to a really old shrunken man who's just walked in with a walking frame. The man has a pointy face and absolutely no hair, except for a few whiskers under his sharp nose. He twitches and rubs at his nose with the back of his hands from time to time. He reminds me of a mouse.

I whisper to Mum that I want to sit down. Mouse-dude turns to me and says in Chinese, "I gave your Por Por her first job when she was 18. She was so quick and smart. You look a lot like her when she was young. Did you know she was the only one in her family to go to high school? Worked so hard at the factory. Ah Mei-Lan, she made some changes in that old factory, yes she did…"

Then he says a few words I don't know, so I glance at Mum, letting her know with my look that I didn't quite understand that last bit.

"I'll tell you later," Mum says. "Why don't you sit down now and take a break? You've been such a great help."

I smile at Mum and nod goodbye to Mouse-dude. I take Mum's crumpled tissue and swap it with a fresh one from the packet I was holding in my hands. She nods gratefully, gently pats my cheek and I walk to the back of the room where I find a row of chairs that have been pushed away to make the room bigger. I sit down and scan the room. I can see Dad by the windows speaking to some of Por Por's friends. They are her knitting crew and they're sitting in a little semi-circle knitting. It's what Por Por loved to do, making her gorgeous colourful jumpers and shawls, so her crew decided to honour her today doing just that.

They're talking about Por Por's friend Goldie.

"Poor Goldie, she couldn't come."

"Yes, she told me her doctor wouldn't let her fly because of her hip operation. At our age, these things take forever to heal. My knees took six months to feel normal again!"

"You know Goldie used to live in Hong Kong? University, I think, no, maybe high school. I don't remember. Not just the hips or knees, the memory's gone too... Goldie was devastated not to be here."

"Life can throw you some big punches."

Then they flip to talk in Chinese so I stop listening.

I look at my watch. We've been in the function centre for hours now. Mum and Great-Aunt Lily set up the carnations and food this morning. They've been cooking for two days. A big table in the middle of the room is laid out with a roast pig and duck, a special Chinese veggie dish and a big bowl of steamed rice. Earlier on, they squabbled about which bowl was the nicer one to use. Seeing the pretty blue ceramic bowl on the table, it seems silly now.

A fruit platter with lychees and tiny mandarins add pops of bright orange and red onto the table. They remind me of one of Por Por's knitted jumpers. Por Por's favourite fruit is lychee. She is the best lychee peeler. One time we had a competition and she peeled 15 lychees to my six. I can see her in my mind when she won, whooping and running around the living-room in a lap of honour!

Then on the side of the table, we placed some tea and wine. Incense sticks stand among the dishes, with its smoky wisps summoning our relatives' ancestral spirits to come and help in the next journey.

I open my backpack and look inside. When Dad and I arrived in Hong Kong, Mum was waiting for us at the airport. She had a big smile on her face even though she stood slouched and kept rubbing her eyes. I noticed her hair was in a bun – she only ever ties it up like that when she thinks her hair is dirty and she doesn't have time to wash it. But she looked so happy to see me and I was so happy to see her! She gave me the biggest hug and a bag of things she got for me for this trip. One of these things is a new journal.

I take the journal out of my backpack and start writing.

Alyssa's journal

Today I'm grateful for...

- Mum and Dad. Although they fight and don't live together any more, they are here for me and for each other. Mum once said to me no one's family looks exactly like another's. All that's important is we love each other in our own way.

- Endless family and friends who keep coming in through the door! I love that Por Por has touched so many people.

- Great-Aunt Lily and Por Por were very close. I'm glad they had time together this year. I'm going to speak to Great-Aunt Lily more this trip about Por Por's life and what she was like as a little girl. I wonder when she started making her own clothes?

- Getting a juicy and sweet lychee. So delicious. The juice trickled down my hand when I peeled off the shell and I had to lick it up quickly.

- No one seeing me licking lychee from my hand!

Quote of the day

"You can't connect the dots looking forward;
you can only connect them looking backwards.
So you have to trust that the dots will
somehow connect in your future."

Steve Jobs

Fake Snake

Ellie

I upload my latest clip, Shake, Make and Bake. I'm dancing and singing in the kitchen while whisking and making choc-chip cookies. I flip my high-pony hair in an oversized sequin scrunchie, and twirl in Mum's baby-pink apron, mixing the batter and adding chocolate chips. Instructional and entertaining! I feel happy that I did a good job with this one. I take a cookie. Might as well eat them, since I made them.

And that's when it starts. Just after I post. Ding, the little envelope icon pops up… a direct message.

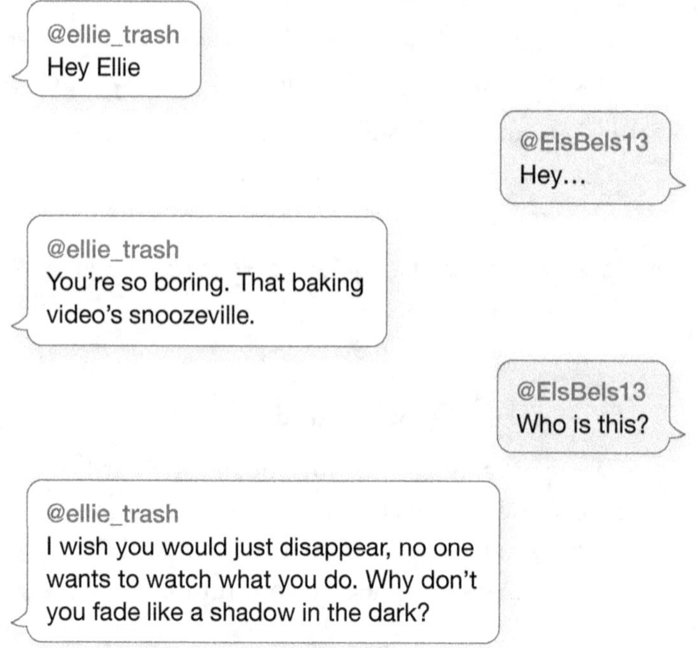

The heart icon next to the Shake, Make and Bake post fills up with rainbow colour but I can't get past these messages. My palms start to sweat as I close the app. I drop my phone onto the bed.

Why would anyone write that? Who are they? They even have my name in their account name. Weird. Scary. Do I know them?

As I hop off the bed, I accidentally kick my satchel bag. All my stuff spills out onto the floor – a shell that I loved so much I kept it to remind me to take a deep breath, a photo of Lys and me taken on the first day of preschool, a notebook and pencil for moments of inspiration, my compact mirror (comes in handy when you want to check your hair before a video or shine light into your enemy's eyes!), a little money purse Lys's Por Por knitted for me and my sunglasses. All these things are really important to me and have helped me through so many sticky situations – I forgot they were there.

I shove all the stuff back safely into my satchel, hoist it onto my shoulder and put the sunglasses on with trembling hands.

"Mum, I'm heading to the park. Back in an hour!" I call.

Lucy peeks her head out of her room and she starts to say something, but changes her mind when she senses my mood. She probably wants to tag along. She always wants to tag along.

I walk the block towards the park deep in thought. The mean messages on FunStar really shook me. The messages are still rattling in my head, weighing down my stomach. I walk faster, trying to erase them from my head and heart. It's probably some random kid who thinks it's funny. Maybe it was a dare and that's it. I think my posts are okay. It's just me and my friends having fun.

One of the swings is free so I sit on it. It's been so long since I've been on a swing. My butt feels a bit snug on the child-size seat. Seriously, they need to make adult-size swings. I pump my legs up and down, feeling the breeze in my hair. I lean back to get a little higher. To feel the breeze a little more. I tilt my head back to look at the world upside down. How weird everything looks. Topsy-turvey place. Feels a bit like that at the moment. Higher and higher I swing, sitting upright now looking towards the familiar scene of my street and my house among the jacaranda trees, gently swinging until I forget what's bothering me.

Aunty Jam

Lucy

Mum and Dad finally unground me and let me stay at Aunty Jam's for the weekend, although my device is still grounded at Dad's work. Aunty Jam is Dad's sister. But they are as different as mermaids and dragons. Aunty Jam is a mermaid, wrapped in a cozy blanket, with a bunch of flowers and a cupcake.

I grab my large shoulder bag that I use for sleepovers and throw in stuff for my weekend away with Aunty Jam. I've done this so many times now, I have my packing sorted:

- 4 × underwear in plain colours. I don't like the ones with ice creams or love hearts or with bows. Just black, blue and white for me.

- 2 × t-shirts

- 1 × pair of shorts with pockets

- 1 × dress with pockets

- 1 × hoodie with pockets

- 1 × comfy pjs and you guessed it with pockets (everything's better with pockets)

- koala hairbrush and my toothbrush. I can use Aunty Jam's toothpaste.

BEEP, beep, beeppp, BEEP beeppp. I hear Aunty Jam out the front. I run and give Mum and Dad a kiss goodbye and I'm off. Bag over my shoulder, I skip to the car.

"Hi, Aunty Jam!" I call through the window.

"Love your hair, Lucy! That's a great colour!" I smile for the first time since being grounded as I jump in the back of the car.

I love spending the weekend with Aunty Jam. I go to her place every holiday for a weekend. It's our special time together. We always do interesting things. She also knows everything. Like how to boil an egg without it cracking, how to make yummy cookies without a recipe, how to make unicorn slime and where to find frogs. Yep, she knows everything and she wears the best clothes from the secondhand shop.

Aunty Jam lives about five songs away. I don't have a watch so I count everything by songs. It goes by in a flash as we chat away about everything: the birds that we see in the garden, when it's going to rain, what makes it rain, how bushfires come in the summer. We talk about the ocean and the mountains. Aunty Jam tells me that when clouds are dark grey, they are rain clouds. How it feels colder just before it rains. I'm going to pay attention next time it rains.

We arrive at Aunty Jam's house. She lives in a semi, which is half a house. Her half is painted green and she has a blue door. Her flowers are always blooming. I tell her I want to live in the other half when I grow up. She laughs and helps me put my bag in the room up the front.

Her cat Benjamin sees me and does a curly circle around my leg to say hello. He is fluffy and soft. I give Benjamin a huge cuddle and we pad out together to the kitchen.

I pull myself up onto a stool at the kitchen bench while Aunty Jam makes pancakes. She makes the best pancakes; her secret ingredient is shredded apple. It makes them sweet and juicy. Just thinking about them makes my mouth water. Yum. I flick through one of Aunty Jam's garden magazines lying on the kitchen bench. Aunty Jam puts a pile of small pancakes in front of me. I pick one up and toss it from one hand to the other impatiently. Ouchie, still too hot to eat.

I like looking at all the pretty gardens and flowers in the magazine. White flannel flowers, purple hydrangeas, pink proteas. Aunty Jam has taught me what all the different flowers are called. The magazine has an article at the back on how to make a compost bin in your own garden.

"Aunty Jam, look at this. We've been learning about composting at school. We have a big pile in the corner of our school garden!"

"Tell me about it," says Aunty Jam.

"We have a special garden bed in the sun where we put our food scraps from lunch and the canteen. It's covered by a piece of cloth. Sometimes during class, we go out and rake it to mix it all up – all full of worms and centipedes. You can see them wriggle when you rake. Mr Higgins also says it's full of things we can't see like bacteria and fun, fun… I think he called it… fun-dust? We put the compost on our herb and vegetable garden at school to help things grow. Mr Higgins says it's all part of the eco-thingy and how we give good food back to the plants."

"Most of the rubbish that we put in the bin can be used as compost," says Aunty Jam.

I nod. Aunty Jam knows everything. "Composting also means we don't need to use as much fertiliser or water in the garden. It's a cool, natural way to keep the plants healthy," Aunty Jam explains.

"Aunty Jam, can we make one for your garden? I'd like your plants to be happy too!" I say.

"Yes, I've been thinking I should do a compost bin for a little while now. Let's do it. Lucy, can you read that article so we know what we need to do?"

"Already on it," I say, ripping out the article.

"We need a plastic bin with a lid, a drill, soil, dried leaves, food scraps, shredded newspapers and a spray bottle with water."

"I think we have all of those things," says Aunty Jam, grabbing a newspaper off the table and heading for the garden shed. Benjamin and I follow her into the backyard. Aunty Jam starts banging and crashing. Stuff flies out of the shed and onto the lawn. A bin, a lid, something like a sack of potatoes. I giggle.

"There," she says. Aunty Jam's face is bright red and she is holding a drill in her hands. She admires the pile she has made on the lawn and I clap my hands together. Benjamin thinks this is way too dirty for him and climbs onto her deck chair in the sun to watch us instead.

"What now?"

I pull the folded article out of my pocket. See, always good to have pockets.

Seven steps to make a compost bin

1. Drill 9 holes into the bin about 3cm apart.

2. Put the shredded newspaper into the bin, filling up a quarter of the bin.

3. Add soil until the bin is half full. Top it off with a layer of dried leaves.

4. Add a layer of food scraps. Use fruit and vegetable scraps – nothing animal.

5. Put the lid on, turn your bin on the side and roll it around.

6. Take the lid off and spray the compost with just enough water to get things damp but not soaking wet. Put the lid back on.

7. Keep adding to your compost, keeping the same balance of soil and leaves. Mix once a week.

We carefully follow each of the steps. It turns out that the sack of potatoes is actually soil. Aunty Jam rakes up the dry gum leaves off her lawn and layers them like a blanket in the compost bin. We both push the bin over and roll it around. Aunty Jam sings loudly, "Roll, roll, roll your bin, gently as it spins. Merrily, merrily, merrily composting begins."

I join in to sing it again, louder, as we stand the bin up after a good mix.

"Hope the neighbours don't mind our loud singing!" I laugh.

"Gah, I never care what the neighbours think of me! They know me well enough by now, don't you, Gerald?" Aunty Jam shouts in case her neighbour, Gerald, is listening.

I fill up the spray bottle at the outside tap and spray all over the top of the compost. I spray a bit on my face too since it's getting hot out here. Aunty Jam gestures at her face, so I spray her grinning sweaty-pink face.

"Yay, our compost will be ready in six weeks!" I say, stuffing the instructions back into my pocket.

Aunty Jam says it's time for a cup of tea. I get a nice cold drink of water with ice. We wash our hands and I sit down on the deck table and chairs outside with Benjamin who rolls his eyes at me and shifts a smidgen to make room, while Aunty Jam makes her cup of tea inside.

"That was so fun and easy. Benjamin, don't you think everyone should have a compost bin?" Benjamin wiggles closer and purrs.

The letters

Alyssa

Great-Aunt Lily lives in a tiny teeny unit in Orchard Terrace. Mum's been living there for the three months she's been in Hong Kong looking after Por Por. There are two bedrooms, a kitchen and one main living-room area which has one table with four chairs. That's it. When I first came to the unit, I was surprised by how neatly Great-Aunt Lily lives. Everything has a place and she doesn't have anything she doesn't need. One saucepan, one frying pan, two plates, two bowls and two mugs. The kitchen has one kettle, one electric cooking plate and one small rice cooker. A bunch of wooden chopsticks sit in a glass jar looking like a modern flower display. It surprises me because I had it in my mind that all old people have a mess of things collected throughout their life, like Por Por's unit in Australia! How funny the two sisters live so differently.

We're getting Mum's things. She and I are moving into a hotel together because there's no room here for me. Mum and Great-Aunt Lily work in one of the bedrooms packing clothes into a suitcase. There's no space to move around so I wait in the living-room looking at the bookcase. There's one black and white photo, yellowing on the edges, of four kids standing in front of an old building. There are three girls and one boy. All of them are grinning in tatty looking t-shirts and shorts or skirts. I pick up the photo to get a closer look at the kids to see if I can tell which one is Por Por, when my elbow knocks a tin box off the bookshelf. The box falls onto the floor with a loud clatter.

"I'm okay! I just knocked an old moon cake box off the bookshelf. Nothing's broken!" I reassure Great-Aunt Lily.

The box is the usual square tin box that moon cakes come in for the Mid-Autumn Festival. Mmm, I love moon cakes, the pastry is soft, the inside is sweet and yummy. This tin's pretty old, dented here and scratched there, in faded red and gold. The lid fell off on the way down from the bookshelf, its contents spilling out. On the floor I see a Dr Who bookmark, a brochure with a plane on the front, a concert ticket to see Barbra Streisand in December 1979, some black and white school photos clipped together with a rusted paper clip and a whole bunch of old well-read letters.

I kneel down on the floor to gather up the items, then stop my tidying to take a better look at the class photos. There's the teacher. An English-looking man with bushy eyebrows wearing a shirt and tie, and there's a girl in the front row with curly frizzy hair who is also English-looking. She has one arm over the shoulders of another girl who has short black straight hair, round glasses, and who looks a bit like me! They both look around my age, maybe a couple of years older. They're smiling at the camera, heads tilted towards each other, wearing the same simple tunic uniform.

I rifle through the letters next – the oldest letter I can see is from 1968 when Por Por would have been 18 years old. I pick up one of these letters and start reading.

Martha Goldsmith
9 Sandyview Street
Quiet Meadows, Australia

13 July 1968

Mei-Lan Lee
Flat 17, Block 9 Community Flats
1827 Orchard Terrace
Kowloon, Hong Kong

To my dear friend Mei,

Flying is both the most wonderful and frightening experience in the world! Wowzers, it blew my mind!

At first I felt anxious. My tummy was churning in a way I have never felt before. I don't want to gross you out writing this, but we have spoken of many things, and here is another. I nearly threw up. I was so nauseous, I had this feeling of wanting to throw up, but never actually did.

Father was sitting next to me and I saw him take deep breaths. I copied him and took deep breaths of my own to try to calm down and realised the breathing really helped.

It really settled my nerves for sure. Once my heartbeat slowed down, I was thinking straight again. I realised I'm safe and I'm going to be right as rain. In fact, I thought to myself, why not enjoy the moment?

So the next time the plane bopped up and down, I whooped and imagined I was rocking out at a Rolling Stones concert! The plane was dancing as I was dancing. That made me less anxious.

In case you were wondering back in the safety of your home in Hong Kong, clouds don't enter the plane (this is what they call the cabin) – it has something to do with the room being pressurised. We fly so high you cannot even see the birds! It was so rad, I was over the moon. Well, not literally. You get my drift.

I will only tell this to you, as you are my friend who understands how I feel – someone who has known me for the last six of my eighteen years on Earth.

Honestly, I have been thinking about this since arriving back in Australia.

I'm not sure about going to teaching college here and becoming a teacher.

There. I have put that down on paper now. Goodness. Everyone, including you, knows that I am destined to become a teacher. Because Father is truly a great teacher. Which, of course, you know because he taught you for many years at our school in Hong Kong. And I have learnt many things from him. It's just that everyone seems to expect I become a teacher without even questioning it. I don't know, Mei. I know it's very disrespectful to think otherwise.

After being on the aeroplane, it dawned on me that there are so many places and so many things out there for us! I spoke to the pilot on the aeroplane. He said that there are no female pilots and he even laughed when I asked him. He asked, "Why would you want to do something so hard? There is a lot of training. Perhaps you could become an air stewardess instead."

Look, he was kind, but he really bugged me. I want more and I'm frustrated. It doesn't seem fair, does it?

Got me thinking, though. What if I start by being an air stewardess? Then I will become a pilot. Then I can get an aeroplane and fly wherever I want to go. Whenever I want to go. I'll be like a bird! I know I can do it.

Tell me more about your new boss, Mr Mouse. I would like to meet him one day, a mousy man sounds like my kind of man! I can boss him around. Ha ha!

Mei, let me tell you another thing. I've decided I do not want to marry. I know it is expected of me and I know Father will be disappointed – probably because he thinks a husband can look after me. Gah, I can look after myself!

I am so very proud of you for getting a job. I want to hear all about it. I know you envy my studies, but it is you I envy. I wish I were working and making money. Then I could have more independence – I so want to live how I want to live. I am sick of all the expectations of me, of us as women, of not being able to do whatever the heck we want.

Right now, I need to figure out how to get out of teaching college. Help me, Mei, you are my only conspirator!

Your friend all the way on the other side of the world!

Martha

Martha Goldsmith
9 Sandyview Street
Quiet Meadows, Australia

12 April 1969

Mei-Lan Lee
Flat 17, Block 9 Community Flats
1827 Orchard Terrace
Kowloon, Hong Kong

Dear Mei,

G'day from my back porch! I'm writing to you today watching the black cockatoos flying from tree to tree as the sun sets over the hill. Very chilled.

In your last letter you said you were working very hard and that your boss, Mr Mouse has asked you to pick up the payroll work. Whoopee - that's incredible. You were always a gun with numbers. I've been thinking about that thing at your work - that doesn't make sense to me either. I'll have a good think about it and write to you again.

How's Lily going with her English? Did you teach her from that book I sent you? You'll see I included some comic books in this package. They're for both of you. They're super funny and the pictures will help Lily understand the English better so she can read them aloud to you. She will get there!

35

I also bought you some patterns I picked up at the shops. The lady says these psychedelic tops are the way to go these days. I don't know, not for a practical chick like me, but I know you like knitting so give them a go! Don't forget we're opposite seasons here in Australia — we have summer at the end of the year, so don't send me any of your knitted things until June!

Not much news from me. Officially done with my first term at teaching college but still yearning for the skies! I've been doing some research and when I'm 20 years old, I can apply to be an air stewardess. It's not far away now. I've been borrowing a lot of books from the library about how aeroplanes fly. It's awesome. And serving tea to people politely when they visit to practise serving tea properly. I know that will make you laugh because who knew I could serve tea, but I'm really serious about this.

Father and I have a bit of a routine now. We left Hong Kong because of his Headmaster role at the boys' grammar school, and that is going so well for him. I'm glad. He is very busy and so I'm at home alone most evenings and weekends. I do my studies, read about aeroplanes, I'm studying physics on the side, I write to you and meet some of my college friends here and there and go to the movies.

One of the boys from college has been asking me out and I've been to the movies with him a couple of times

(so I don't have to talk to him!). He is very boring.
I asked him about aeroplanes and what he thinks
about flying them and he told me people can die flying
around too much. He thinks we should just stay at
home and watch the telly.

I hope you are having more luck in that department
than me!

Love, Martha

Mistakes

Ellie

Even having my phone in my pocket these days makes my heart pound. I haven't posted anything recently. I'm scared there might be a string of nasty messages from @ellie_trash. I don't know what this person might say to me. So much for "Fun" Star. I glance at my phone. Five new followers. I feel empty. This used to bring me so much joy. Why am I trusting people I don't know? Why am I sharing so much about me? What am I doing that caused this? FunStar didn't come with warnings. Beware of sharks! All these questions swimming in my head.

I think the worst part of it is that I don't know who it is. It could be anyone. It could even be someone I know. I shudder. If I know who it is, I can at least do something about it, like what Lys did with Daniel at soccer when we were in primary school. He would call us names and have his gang make fun of us less-good players. Lys was so brave. Stood up to him. I miss Lys.

But I don't know who this is. I don't even know who to say stop to. It's useless. I'm getting these messages every few days.

Ding. A direct message.

Ding. A second message.

I don't want to look. But the envelope icon is blinking and I can't help myself.

@DanielSoccer
Hi Ellie. It's Daniel…

@DanielSoccer
From soccer last year

@ElsBels13
Hey Daniel. We haven't seen each other in so long! I stopped soccer.

@DanielSoccer
Yeah, I know. You and Alyssa both stopped.

@ElsBels13
What's up?

@DanielSoccer
I found you on FunStar. Your posts are ok.

@ElsBels13
Thanks. How's the All Stars Team going?

@DanielSoccer
Oh yeah, on that …

@ElsBels13
I didn't bother putting my name down. I think Lys did though, although she never got to try out.

@DanielSoccer
Yeah I know. Hey, actually it's about that...

@ElsBels13
The All Stars Team?

@DanielSoccer
Yeah. Look, I did something that coach said I had to sort out. I don't have her number. Can you give it to me?

@ElsBels13
Oh

@DanielSoccer
Alyssa put her name down on the list to try out. I crossed her name off because I didn't think she was good enough for the team.

@ElsBels13
Oh, that's not cool.

@DanielSoccer
I know, I know. Coach said I can't continue in the All Stars team unless I'm a team player. It was really stupid of me. We also lost nationals this year. Made me think a lot.

@ElsBels13
Look, Lys and I are actually not talking as much as we used to and I don't think I can give her number to you without her ok. I'll ask her for you.

@DanielSoccer
Ok, thanks

With that, he's offline. I close the app and sit at my desk thinking. That was interesting. I open up my laptop and look at my last email to Lys, inviting her to my birthday party. Urghh, I sound so self-absorbed. All about FunStar and Josie and Ruby. What's with me?

I grab my bag and take out the photo of me and Lys when we were at preschool. Then I open my photos folder on my laptop and go through all the other 1,897 photos I have which are tagged Lys. Here we are on the roller-coaster at the Easter Show screaming at the top of our lungs with our eyes squeezed shut. Here's that time our tongues turned blue from the cheap lollies we got at Halloween and here we are in Aunty Jam's backyard toasting marshmallows.

I need to talk to her. I need her help with what's happening with FunStar. I need to tell her about the soccer list. It wasn't because Coach didn't think she was good enough! I want to tell her all about Lucy's crazy composting obsession. Oh, and that cookie recipe was not bad too.

With tears in my eyes I bring up the mail program and start typing. As I write I realise I don't even know what she's doing this summer. We've stopped speaking for six months now. That's a long time. I look down at my hands and sigh. I realise among all the things I need to tell her, I need to say sorry too.

Composting continued

Lucy

I'm obsessed with composting. I've learnt that compost saves water by helping the soil hold moisture and it reduces rubbish by reusing our food scraps. Who would have thought composting could be so awesome? And it's all rubbish! Just good old rubbish helping out. Even rubbish is useful.

I sit down on the computer at home to do some more research on composting and look at the search list that pops up. I've read that one and that one. Okay, next page.

I click on a video and a picture of a lyrebird pops up. A serious deep voice starts talking.

"The composting lyrebird.

"The lyrebird, more readily known for its magical singing and ability to mimic the sounds of other birds, tractor noises or even a car alarm, may have a secret strength. The lyrebird plays a key role as a composter in the Australian bush ecosystem. This unlikely composter speeds up the decomposition process of bushland litter, not unlike the way you may compost in your garden. The lyrebird's foraging ability and rake-like feet speeds up the composting process. The lyrebird can reduce forest litter by an outstanding amount. So why is this so important? This composting can create unburnt and protected patches in large bushfires. These patches become safe havens for other animals to survive."

I scroll down to the script below the video and send it to print. I grab the printout off the printer to show Ellie. I know Ellie has seen lyrebirds at Blue Lake. She has always said they were magical.

"Ellie," I call. "You've got to see this."

"What?" Ellie calls back from her room. "I'm busy. I'm writing an email."

I knock on her door and wait patiently. It's hard. I usually just open it because who can be bothered waiting? But I realise if I need Ellie's help, I need to play by her rules. I wait. I pick at a mozzie bite on my arm as I wait. Wish I had a song to listen to while I wait.

Finally, Ellie opens the door. "Why are you bothering me?" she asks.

I show her the article which Ellie reads standing by her door. "What does this mean?" I ask her.

Her eyes light up and she smiles. "Wow, they are even more extraordinary than I imagined. So cool. They can help save animals' lives in bushfires. Amazing. Although I shouldn't be amazed. Ayrebirds, I mean, lyrebirds are super cool creatures..."

She looks a little far away and she tells me to come into her room. I shrug, this is new, but I go in and plop onto her bed. Ellie turns to her desk and saves the draft email she was writing before closing her laptop.

She starts opening her drawers randomly. She rummages through a jewellery box, mutters something then goes to her old backpack sitting at the back of her wardrobe. She opens a few zipped pockets, throwing out an old tissue and a muesli bar wrapper onto the carpet. She takes a look at her desk, and finally she says, "I remember!"

Ellie is taking forever. I stare around her room – she has so many nice things, more than me. But I like her art piece the best – she made this amazing sketch of two kookaburras and it was so good that it won a prize.

She searches for something under her bed and pulls out a tin box that used to hold bickies. She opens the box and takes out a gold necklace with a feather on it. It shimmers. Glows even. Ellie cradles it gently in her hands and smiles.

"Can you keep a secret?" she asks.

I nod eagerly. This is Lucy's Rule #16 – keep your sister's secrets or there will be consequences.

"Remember when Lys and I got lost in the bush during a camping trip a couple of years ago? You were little then and were asleep back at the campsite when it happened, but Mum and Dad had to look for us. Well, we saw something magical in those woods by Blue Lake and here is proof. This golden feather shows us that nature has a way of helping each other. I'd almost forgotten. This is a magical feather."

That's a secret worth keeping!

"Tell me more about the composting," Ellie says. "Did you say you made a compost bin at Aunty Jam's? What else did she tell you about the birds and the bushfires in the area?"

Ellie puts her necklace around her neck and we talk well past my bedtime.

More letters

Alyssa

The lights are off in the hotel room I share with Mum. We've had a busy day sightseeing as we want to see as much as we can before we go back to Australia in a few days' time. Mum's spirit has lifted and she gets excited showing me things she remembers from her own limited time in Hong Kong. Some things are not where she remembers them and we laugh at the old and the new as we discover them together. Dad joins us too and it's a great time as a family.

I love the busyness. There's a lot of traffic and people everywhere. The city noise is mechanical – a horn honking, people's phones ringing, the swish of the metro train door closing on you if you're not watching. The food is amazing! I've been trying so many new flavours and I now have some new favourite dishes. Definitely one more bubble egg waffle before we go home, and we know exactly the place to get it. I've tried so many now, I've become an egg-spert!

Once I hear Mum breathing deeply and evenly, I turn to Por Por's old moon cake tin which I left on the floor next to my bed. When I realised what was in the box, I asked Great-Aunt Lily about it. She told me she's a Buddhist and tries to follow minimalism principles.

"Living in a small home helps," she joked.

As she was the only one of her siblings living in the family home, she told everyone they were allowed only one box to put anything they wanted to keep. Otherwise she'd throw everything out! Por Por kept some letters and a few mementos. Great-Aunt Lily gave Mum and me Por Por's box to keep.

I haven't had much time to figure out what each item meant to Por Por, but I love looking at the letters the most. I feel close to Por Por as I imagine her receiving these stories from her best friend Martha. Por Por in a cramped bedroom in Hong Kong among all its bustling noises and in contrast, Martha sitting on her porch looking out into the wide open spaces of greens and browns, with only the birds twirping in the background and the occasional gust of wind.

I think of Ellie and me, and wish we were friends again. I can imagine that we are in the 1960s writing letters to each other, laughing about boys and classes and the movies we've been watching.

I turn on the torch on my phone to find a letter to read.

Martha Goldsmith
9 Sandyview Street
Quiet Meadows, Australia

21 August 1970

Mei-Lan Lee
Flat 17, Block 9 Community Flats
1827 Orchard Terrace
Kowloon, Hong Kong

Dear Mei,

I had to write to you! Last month I saw an advert in Father's newspaper looking for air stewardesses. It read: "Girls who want to go places get their start at McConnell Airline School."

Of course I want to go places. I want to fly an aeroplane! I want to see the mountain of Kilimanjaro and the beaches in the south of France. I want to dance with Mick Jagger and sing at the Opera House. So I rang the McConnell Airline School.

Miss McConnell herself answered the phone. She had a breathy voice and kept calling me honey or sugar or sweetie. At first she was quite nice, asking me why I was interested and we talked about my wanting to see the world. Then to my horror, she asked a bunch of really personal questions. She asked if I had a boyfriend, how tall I am and whether I had a "neatly proportioned figure". Those were her exact words.

Miss McConnell said I had to be between 5'2" and 5'9" and weigh between 105 to 135 pounds and be in proportion to height.

I laughed and said, "I reckon I'm in proportion, I mean, my arms fit into my shirts and I can get into my jeans pretty easily."

I meant it as a friendly way to answer her somewhat rude questions but she was no fun.

There was a long pause on the phone, then she breathed, "My dear, you better come into my office so I can check you out for myself."

So a few days later, I went to see Miss McConnell.

I had butterflies in my stomach. I don't know how much I weigh. I have lived with Father all my life. I don't know anything about cosmetics or lipstick or what clothes to wear that bring out the best in my figure. I don't even care for my figure. Mei, I didn't know what to do.

Oh, but I wanted to get somewhere. If women can't be pilots, this was at least something I could do as a first step.

It was a disaster. When I saw Miss McConnell, she looked me up and down. She measured my height, she made me step on some scales. She actually touched my hair! Then I had to balance a book on my head and walk around the room. I dropped it a few times.

But the worst moment was when the belt loop on my
dress got caught on a trolley and all the cups of tea
I was pretending to serve to fake dummy customers
fell off the trolley! Black tea and milk splashed
everywhere! I mean everywhere! On to the dummy, on to
her floor and I am sure I stained her perfect white
tablecloth...

I never felt so humiliated in my life. I tried to grab
a cloth and mop up everything, but ended up knocking
a stool over in the process. I stopped then. It was no
use, I am a klutz!

Miss McConnell was not impressed. In her breathy
voice, she told me to sit down (on the stool which I put
back upright). She told me my dress was adequate
and I seemed sensible enough, but my goodness where
did I get my shoes? They were my tennis shoes! Super
comfy and much better than those Mary-Jane buckle
shoes all the girls are wearing at my teaching college.
Besides, I didn't own a pair.

She sighed. Yes, she sighed. Then she said this, "Honey,
we can't accept you. You're just not... stewardess
material."

"I can practise all the tea serving and be better..."
I pleaded. I was crestfallen.

"You're sweet. You have lovely manners and are genuine.
That I can't fault you. But this is a glamorous job.

We need spark! We need pizzazz! We need glitter! Our customers expect our girls to be all of that. You're a little heavier than what we would take in and well..."

"You hate my shoes, don't you?"

Darling, hate is a strong word. Of course, I don't hate your shoes. I myself have a pair for tennis. I do have a mild dislike for the combination - who wears sneakers with a dress? What is the world coming to? Tsk, tsk. Sweetie, we have standards."

There was nothing more I could say after that.
I didn't meet their standards.

Martha

I rummage through the box for the next letter after this one. I'm desperate to know what happens next. But I can't find it! That's strange, I think. I grab the box and tip-toe quickly to the bathroom so I can close the door and turn on the light. Once in the bathroom, I flick through the letters and sort them in chronological order. It looks like some are missing.

The next proper letter I can find is dated December 1971. Martha talks about finishing her teaching college and a graduation ceremony. There's nothing more about being an air stewardess though. I really hope she's become one! Please don't give up.

I find some birthday cards dated in the late 1970s from both Martha and Mr Goldsmith that wish Por Por a happy birthday with some generic well-wishing message but nothing more. They all have a funny saying on the front or a silly photo.

It's getting late so I decide to go to bed and look through the other letters at another time. As I grab the lid to the box, I notice a card sticking to the inside of the lid. I peel it off gently so the colour ink doesn't peel off onto the tin. There's a beautiful drawing of a girl on the front of the card. She's climbing a mountain, determined and strong. You can't see the top, just snow and trees, all mystical and dreamy. She's just climbing, happy, on a mission, maybe she doesn't care if she reaches the top or not. Maybe it doesn't matter to her. I flip the card over and there's Martha's familiar handwriting.

Dear Mei,

I met a fortune teller who read tarot cards in Paris! She tells me I'm an adventurer. I know she can tell I'm not French... but still I want to believe it. I will believe it. I am an adventurer.

Did you know the word "courage" is derived from the French word "coeur", which means heart? Speak from the heart. Follow your heart. Do what you love. These are all the things I've been learning lately.

Love, Martha

Bird home

Lucy

Summer holidays can get a bit boring. You know, like nothing to do. Staying at home. Reading books. I've watched the same dragon movie now like 10 times. Seriously. Enough. I flick off the movie with the remote and slide off the couch.

I put my hands on my hips and tap my feet. Mum has banned me from the food colouring or any of her things since the pink hair incident. I look at my beautiful pink hair shining back at me in the reflection of the TV screen. I still love it.

I start opening all the kitchen cupboards. Flour, rice, breakfast cereal. Nope, nothing. I stomp down the hall to Ellie's room and grab the *Fun Activities for Rainy Days* book off her shelf. I sit down on the edge of Ellie's bed. Slime (done that), bath bombs (been there), origami dogs (urgh).

Maybe something outside. I walk back down the hall and straight out the back door. Skipping rope, handball, dirty frisbee (sigh).

I look up and see a pair of beautiful red and green birds in the tree. Their chest and body are a beautiful bright red. Their beaks are pink and their wings the colour of the trees. Amazing. Wow!

The birds are making a loud high-pitch whistle and I turn and see a few more birds in another tree in our neighbour's backyard. I've never seen these types of birds before! And here are a pair in our backyard and a few more over there. They're so beautiful.

I go back inside, the *Fun Activities for Rainy Days* book is still sitting on the coffee table. I'm about to pack it up so Ellie won't know I sneaked into her room without her knowing, when the open pages catch my attention. The activity is building a birdhouse! Perfect!

I skip around the house and rummage for what I can find. First stop, the recycling. Little and big cardboard boxes, a tube, plastic containers. I scoop them up and throw them on the rug on the lounge-room floor.

The bathroom cupboards. I push the hair dye out of the way. Cotton wool, Mum's white towels. The nice fluffy ones. Why should birds use the old crusty hard towels? Maybe not the nail polish, that can't be good for birds.

The art and craft drawer is full of sticky-tape, scissors, paint, string, paper, permanent markers and a hole puncher.

After a few trips, I spread myself out on the lounge-room floor surrounded by all the stuff.

Okay. I've got this. I grab the big cardboard box. The book says to start with that. I grab the scissors and start cutting off the flaps. I flip the box on its side so it's a bit like a cave. I grab a large round cardboard tube. I cut a hole in the side of the box, then wedge the tube into the side of the box.

This is hard work. Time for a break. I get a big bag of popcorn from the pantry and a bowl. I tug at the bag and pop it open. Popcorn goes everywhere. I look down as it spills on the table and floor. Well, at least some of it lands in the bowl. I scoop a couple of extra handfuls off the table, pick up the bowl and walk back to the lounge. The popcorn on the floor goes crunch under my feet as I go.

I use the scissors to start cutting a fluffy towel into small strips and squares. I secure one plastic tray to the top of the box and two inside. Finishing touches. I get a bottle of water and fill in a tray on top, I put the little bits of towel and cotton wool inside the container in the box. Food! I need food. I rummage through the kitchen cupboards and find sunflower seeds. Perfect. I fill the final plastic tray inside with the seeds.

I slump back against the couch for a moment (with my popcorn) and admire my work. Can't rest for too long. The birds need a home. I pick up the box and squeeze carefully sideways through the sliding door that leads to the backyard. I pop the birdhouse outside on a low tree branch, some of the water spilling out as I wedge it in place. It's a bit wonky but I'm sure the birds won't mind. I hope they like it!

It's nearly dinner-time for me now too, so I go back inside the house. Mum is standing there, hands on her hips, looking at my popcorn littered path and all the strips of towels and cotton balls I left in the lounge-room, on the sofa and around the coffee table. Her face is livid. I don't know why, I was helping the birds in our backyard!

As Mum starts yelling at me to tidy up, I see Ellie sneak past and take a look at my birdhouse outside. She takes away my plastic tray with water on top! She's in the kitchen throwing it in the recycling, when I'm grabbing the dustpan. I see her go to the top cupboard that I can't reach and grab a deeper plastic bowl left over from a birthday party. She fills that up with water and takes it outside and places it on top of the birdhouse. Yeah, that does work better.

Ellie takes some photos with her phone and comes back inside. Silently, she grabs the strips of towels and shoves them into the laundry before Mum figures out they were her good towels. Dinner is ready. We wash our hands and sit down to eat.

I'm supposed to go to bed soon. But as I make my way to the bathroom, Ellie gestures for me to follow her into her room. She shows me some messages on her phone.

I skip to the bathroom. I usually hate brushing my teeth – what's the point, I'm going to eat again tomorrow. I look at myself in the mirror and smile. I see some green bits from the bolognese sauce and decide it's probably good to get rid of that at least. I flick out the green bit with the toothbrush, move the brush around a little bit more. That should do it. Minty fresh.

I hear the cicadas calling outside and I think of the birdhouse. I wonder if those King Parrots are escaping bushfires and think about checking to see if they're eating the seeds. I might need to put more out overnight. I hope the birdhouse helps them and I hope they like it.

Lucy's Rule #6 is to be in bed immediately after brushing teeth. I've never broken that rule before. But there's always a first.

I check that Ellie is still in her room – I can hear some music coming softly behind her door and creep past. The shower's running from Mum and Dad's bathroom and the light is on in the study. Dad's low rumbly laugh echoes out from the door. He's watching the comedian he likes. Everyone's busy. Perfect.

I sneak past quietly. Again, a first. I am never quiet. I slide open the patio screen and step outside. The night is warm and the air smells smoky. It's dark and I can't quite make out the birdhouse until I'm close to it. It's dropped a little to the right, the cardboard sagging. I'm disappointed there doesn't seem to be anything going on. Maybe in the morning the birds will have the seeds for breakfast. I reach out to straighten the droopy side.

A golden flash catches my attention. It must be Ellie with a flashlight. I turn towards it. Nope.

I start walking back towards the house, wishing again for the birdhouse to help all the birds that need water and shelter. Again, something golden swirls quickly in the sky past me.

"Click click."

I spin around. I see some golden dust sprinkled on the grass leading towards the birdhouse. I'm not a sparkles kind of person, but did Ellie add glitter to the birdhouse when she came out?

My eyes follow the gold dust and settle onto a low branch just under the birdhouse. I see a beautiful golden bird perched on the branch. Her eyes glimmer with warmth. She flutters up onto the roof of the birdhouse and balances awkwardly on one foot. I'm worried the birdhouse is going to collapse, but it's holding.

"Chick chock."

Unbelievable

Ellie

In my room with music playing, I sort through my satchel bag. All the things inside have a special meaning to me. I pull out my old notebook and pencil, start to doodle. I haven't been drawing as much recently since I've been on FunStar. I draw a tree with long branches and twirling leaves merging into the sky like smoke. My mind drifts as I shade dark and light tones to create bark. Mr Staples, my art teacher from last year, taught us how to use cross-hatching strokes to create light and dark tones. So cool to have an art teacher whose favourite art style is drawing like mine. I start to colour the sky grey and hazy.

I zone out, adding bits of colour here and there with coloured pencils. It's getting late and I'm tired. I should go to bed soon but I hear Lucy's footsteps patter quickly down our long hallway. Why can't that girl just walk? And why isn't she in bed?

She barges into my room without knocking. Her hair is a mess, sticking to the side of her bright red face.

"The golden bird, Els. It's just like you described her. Glowing, golden, all yellow," she says out of breath.

"She told me the birds need homes. They're thirsty and hungry. We need to help them. She said that animals have been escaping in old wombat burrows for shelter. I was just wishing that the birds would use my house..." she goes on.

"Lucy, are you okay? Slow down," I say.

"Els, Ellie," Lucy says, trying to get control. "It's the Ayrebird. The one you told me about."

I grab Lucy's sweaty palm and we run down the hall. My mind is spinning. It can't be. Lucy's just being silly. That was something magical at Blue Lake ages ago.

"Where, Lucy?" I say, slowing to a walk as I calm down a bit. This birdhouse and composting business surely has gone to her head. She can really get stuck into things.

Lucy stops at the back door and points to her crooked birdhouse in the tree. All I see is darkness and the cardboard house, drooping slightly to the right. There is nothing there. I sigh. I look at Lucy and start to say, "I'm sorry Lucy, but…"

Then Lucy slides open the door and heads outside, pulling me with her by my hand. I shrug and follow her anyway.

As we approach the birdhouse, everything looks normal. I've pretty much decided it's just Lucy and her crazy imagination, when there it is. A small wispy feather just lying there in the birdhouse. It's not just any feather. It's golden and shimmering. Just like the ones Lys and I have. Magical.

Lucy smiles widely as I swoop her up into my arms and give her a cuddle.

"Lucy, you found Aurum. Aurum, the mythical Ayrebird! We've got to tell Lys."

Reunite

From: Ellie Jones
To: Alyssa Tan
Re: Sorry
Thursday 7 January at 9:17pm

Dear Lys,

I'm sorry this email has taken so long for me to send. I know it's been six months and I can't believe we let six months go before I emailed you. I feel awful I let something like a silly app get in the way of our friendship. I've written so many drafts of this email and rewritten it so many times. I really hope I say everything right.

So, about FunStar… it made me feel so loved with all the attention I was getting from followers online. I've been so focused on making these posts. It made me feel good about myself and I realised what I'm good at. I'm sorry I made you feel bad at my birthday party. I'm sorry I didn't reach out sooner. Please don't be mad at me.

I really need you. You know there are bushfires at Blue Lake? They are driving out the birds from there. It's really sad. Aurum needs us. She sent a message via Lucy. I really can't believe it myself but it's true! Lucy made this birdhouse for our backyard and all these birds started coming to it. Including our Aurum.

Lys, Aurum's home is in danger. She helped us get home over a year ago and now we need to help her. I don't know how to do it on my own but you and I together, we're a team!

Love Ellie xx

PS: Miss you

Dear Ellie,

I'm so sorry too! I can never be mad at you, and yes it's been a long time. I've also been meaning to write to you. I've missed talking and sharing things with you. I've been feeling awful too. So many things have happened that I don't know where to begin.

Poor Aurum, this is terrible. I read about the bushfires and I saw there was one near Blue Lake. Are all the wildlife gone from the area? Where can they go? If they are going to your home because of the birdhouse, we must do something. Of course I will help.

Don't worry about your birthday party. I admit I looked down on the app because singing and dancing in front of a camera where others watch you makes me super uncomfortable. Makes me feel not cool enough, unlike you. I should never have made you feel like it was a silly thing. I'm sorry for making you feel that way.

I recently read this quote from my new journal. It's from Winnie the Pooh...

"If ever there is tomorrow when we're not together... there is something, you must always remember. You are braver than you believe, stronger than you seem, and smarter than you think. But the most important thing is, even if we're apart... I'll always be with you."

Isn't that beautiful? We need to remember this.

I have one more really important thing to tell you. It will be a shock to you, so be prepared. Por Por passed away in Hong Kong during her visit. I am devastated. I don't even have the words. Mum and I are feeling a little bit stronger. It's still tough. Little moments can make one of us cry.

Por Por was taken to hospital that night of your birthday party which is why Mum came to get me in the middle of the night.

I'm in Hong Kong now with Mum and Dad. And yes, I need to tell you all about the trip too! We've been here for a few weeks now and we're flying home tomorrow so I'll tell you everything when I get back. And we can make a plan to help poor Aurum and the birds at Blue Lake.

I can meet you at the usual spot on Sunday if that's okay? Like old times?

Love, Lys

Dear Lys,

I am crying as I type. I am so so so sorry. This is the worst news. I love Por Por and I love you. Please, we must promise to keep talking even if we argue and we will, but we must always be there for each other.

And you're in Hong Kong! There is so much we need to talk about. Oh and I have one more thing to tell you… about Daniel but that can wait.

Yes, meet at the usual, 11am at the park. You bring the tissues. I'll bring the choc chip cookies. I have a new recipe.

Love, Ellie xx

Hi Ellie,

We just landed and are on our way home. What do you mean Daniel?! Wow, did he say something mean to you because I'm much louder these days. I will tell him where to go! Please let him not be mean to you on FunStar because that is truly low. He should just let you be.

I'll see you tomorrow. I've been thinking about the birds on the plane and have some ideas but interested in what you're thinking.

Love, Lys

Home

Alyssa

The park where I'm meeting Ellie is small, surrounded by a short pink picket fence. I pace up and down the path that leads from the gate to the swings as I wait. What should I say? How do we start the conversation when it's been so long? Hey Ellie, what's been happening? Or I like your jacket, great colour, is it new? It would be so much easier if we could just push a refresh button, reboot and start again like nothing went wrong. We should never have left speaking for so long. My stomach is doing back flips. What were we thinking, or maybe we didn't think about it enough?

I hear the clink of the park gate and swing around. It's Ellie bouncing along. Looks like she got a new satchel bag! It's swinging about behind her. She runs over to me and we give each other our familiar hug that goes on for a long time. We smile and laugh.

"Ellie, I was..."

"...I know, me too. I don't know..."

"what to say," I finish Ellie's sentence.

"Same," says Ellie.

Seeing Ellie feels like coming home. We pick up where we left off. It is so good to have my go-to-friend back. Despite not speaking for so long we still get each other, and we haven't lost our ability to finish each other's sentences!

"I've been sad with Por Por, you know. First, I missed Mum as she moved to Hong Kong to be with her. And now with Por Por. It's a bit strange though. Sometimes I feel okay and then I feel miserable. Sometimes I lie in bed thinking of her and can't sleep and sometimes I even feel angry that she's gone and that she left us even though I know it's not her fault, of course," I explain.

"Oh, I'm sorry, Lys. I've been so distracted by FunStar. And you know it's not really what I thought it was… it's not great… Anyway, I need to tell you all about Aurum," says Ellie.

"Lucy has become a bit crazy about composting. You know how she gets really into things. She's been collecting all of our apple cores, soggy grapes and carrot peels. She made a compost bin with Aunty Jam. Then she found this really cool article about how lyrebirds are nature's composters. They turn over all the ground with their feet which helps all the leaves breakdown. The amazing thing about this is that it creates safe patches for animals in bushfires as these composted patches don't burn as easily. Can you believe that?"

"Wow, that is so cool."

"I know – so crazy! So then Lucy makes this birdhouse. You know how she loves birds. It's all wonky and saggy, it's made out of cardboard and recycling. But like magic, it works and the birds come. And Aurum visits."

"Oh, Ellie," I say.

"I know, right. Aurum tells Lucy that the birds need help. They need shelter and water."

"We have to help."

"I know – let's do it, Lys!" says Ellie.

At our feet there are yellow dandelions growing in grass mixed with white puffballs of seeds. I pick two puffballs – one for me and one for Ellie. Just like when we were little, we both take a big breath and blow the seeds and make a wish. A wish that we hope will come true. That we will stay true friends forever.

Alyssa's journal

Today I'm grateful for...

- My friendship with Ellie. It's funny how we spent
  six months apart but when we saw each other
  again it was like no time at all had passed.

- Ellie's delicious choc-chip cookies. I ate so many
  I have a tummy-ache.

- Learning the truth about Daniel. I don't know
  how I feel yet. I told Ellie she can give him my
  number. I'm nervous about what he might say to
  me. I really wanted to keep playing soccer, but
  I guess with everything that happened last year,
  I didn't have the time anyway.

- Home. It's nice being home even though I learnt
  so much being away.

Quote of the day

"A friend is one that knows you as you are,
understands where you have been,
accepts what you have become,
and still, gently allows you to grow."

William Shakespeare

Flip flop

Ellie

Things have been a bit up and down for me lately. This morning I was all cosy, comfy and content in bed. That lasted for all of five minutes before Lucy stomped down the hallway waking me up. How rude! Then I just felt annoyed. So I got up and stomped down the hallway too. This made Mum and Dad angry. So we were all stomping around the house and it was only 6:35am on a Monday morning.

Now a bully on FunStar is making me feel really low. After I get a message I can feel flat not for five minutes but for five whole hours.

Ding.

> @ellie_trash
> Watched your post today. Cringe.

Ding.

> @ellie_trash
> Are you always this stupid or are you making a special effort today?

Ding.

> @ellie_trash
> Anyone who told you to be yourself couldn't have given you worse advice.

Tears well up in my eyes. I sigh. But then seeing Lys again. That was the absolute best.

This flip-flopping from happy-sad, angry-calm, irritated-relaxed. It's driving me a bit crazy. At least I have Lys to talk it all out now. That always helps me feel better. Drawing also helps take my mind off things. I get out my pencil and doodle all my moodiness. Mr Staples told us in our last art class that drawing for even ten minutes a day will really improve our skills.

Template

Alyssa

I asked Dad what he would do if something was bugging him about the environment. He said people write to the government and tell them that it's their responsibility to sort these things out. I looked up "writing to the government" on the internet and saw that people can write to the mayor of Blue Lake. There's even an email address. That seemed logical. The government should definitely be doing something about these things.

So Ellie and I wrote an email to the mayor.

From: Alyssa Tan
To: Mayor's Office
Re: Bushfires and concerns for the wildlife
Tuesday 12 January at 11:05am

Dear Mayor,

Our names are Alyssa Tan and Ellie Jones. We are 12 and 13 years old.

At the moment there are bushfires burning. It's on the news, there's a red sun in the sky and there's smoky air every time we step outside. It's making us sad. We're worried about all the birds. The ones who have no shelter or food. The ones who are injured from the fires. We need to take action. The birds need our help. We need your support to:

- plant new trees

- put water containers out

- build shelters

- provide supplies to bird and animal hospitals to help the wounded wildlife.

Please help us to help the birds. We have attached a petition of 23 others who care, too.

Concerned,

Alyssa Tan and Ellie Jones

From: Mayor's Office
To: Alyssa Tan
Re: Bushfires and concerns for the wildlife
Thursday 14 January at 4:05pm

Dear Allie and Eliza,

Thank you for your correspondence dated xxxxxx regarding your concern for the wildlife and protecting the environment.

I have noted your comments and concerns. I, too, feel strongly about helping the animals.

Rest assured, the government will continue to support our animals and the bushland. In fact the government has committed funds to support animal hospitals and shelters.

Through our annual funding program, we also support local bush regeneration programs that remove rubbish from bushland and replant trees. I am optimistic that this will make a positive difference to our environment.

Again, thank you for bringing your concerns to my attention and for caring so much about the environment.

Yours faithfully,

The Mayor

We got the response today and I forwarded it to Ellie straightaway. It was great they wrote back pretty quickly but I couldn't understand what they were saying.

"Ellie, they got our names wrong!" I say when I ring her to ask if she's read the email.

"I'm so annoyed. They didn't even respond to our letter properly," Ellie retorts.

"I know, they just told us what they are already doing. What was the point of that? And what's with the xxxxxx?"

"They couldn't even be bothered to put in the date!" Ellie laughs. "Seriously, I'm so frustrated. Should we write another letter? I'm sorry I laughed but I don't know how to react. Sometimes I laugh when I don't know what to say."

"What's the point? They don't really care about the birds."

"Maybe it's no use. We can't really do anything."

Attack

Ellie

After I hang up with Lys, I flop onto my bed. Writing to the mayor did nothing. We even went around and got 23 signatures from people in our family as well as our neighbours.

It did feel good to be working with Lys again. Once we were talking, Lys and I just got to task. We're good at working together – we dreamed up what we could do to help the birds. We got into action mode. We knocked on doors to get names on the petition and then we wrote the email to the mayor.

I was so busy working with Lys that I pushed aside the thing that had been bothering me. I haven't told Lys yet. If I had thought about it for one second, I should have known the problem wasn't going to just go away. I've been in my own dream world, so happy that Lys and I are talking again that I forgot what was happening on FunStar. I was just ignoring it.

Ding. I snap back to reality. My phone is next to me on my bed and it's flashing with a new notification.

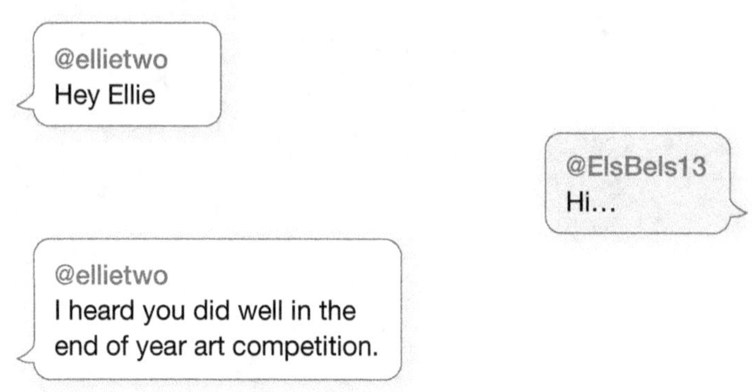

I click on the link and up pops @ellietwo account. There's a whole heap of my videos re-posted but with nasty captions pasted all over the videos.

I can't look away from the site. I know I should but I'm stuck. I frantically start scrolling through the videos. Then the streams of comments. There are so many comments. Some of these comments are from people at school. There's Kate who's in maths class. Sami, who I thought was my friend. It's like a tide of hate rising in my tummy up to my throat. I'm going to be sick.

Yasss

Jelly belly Ellie

#overEllie

You are so right, let's get Ellie offline.

This is so funny. LOL.

Els Smells

#awkward

#overit

2 out of 10

Gosh. Who is this bully? The art competition. Were they in Mr Staples' art class with me? These are not just whispers behind my back. These comments are in plain view for everyone to feed off. An ocean of haters. I feel helpless like when I'm out in the sea and the waves keep coming. Every time you come up for air another big wave comes and dumps you. The crash zone. My emotions are pulling me this way and that. Are my videos stupid?

Maybe I should just dive under the wave for cover. I can wait for the big waves to pass and things to calm down. What can I do? There is no lifeguard on shore to rescue me if I put up my hand. You can't just swim between the flags and know you'll be safe.

I think about throwing away my phone, deleting FunStar. I hold down the app to delete. But I like FunStar. If I quit, then this bully and the mean comments are still going to be out there and the bully will get what they want. This account will still exist even if I delete my own, and I think I'd rather know what was being said about me. At least Mum and Dad can't see the direct messages. But what if they find this shadow account? They will be so mad. They would delete my account and take away my phone for sure. I can't tell them, not yet.

So I continue to tread water. I turn my phone off and throw it in my drawer for now.

self love

"Feeling down, Lys, can you come over and keep me company?"
Tidying up
Waiting for Lys to arrive ...
Lys arrives!
Make breakfast masks!
Ingredients:
Egg yolk
Honey
Olive Oil
Oatmeal
Mask
Breakfast Oatmeal!
Yummy
POWER DOWN
GOOEY! STICKY!
Go for a walk in the sun
Sit under a tree
Have a good night's sleep
Hug! Bye!
YOGA!

Look up

Lucy

A few birds are tweeting around my birdhouse outside. Picking at the seeds, taking sips of water. It would be good to do more. I need to help the birds. Money is what I need! Maybe if I can raise some money, I can give it to an adult who can save the birds? I've seen people at the supermarket collecting money. They hold containers that they shake, and people just put money in. So easy! That's what I'll do.

I grab a jar which has a few coins of my pocket money already at the bottom. I draw a picture of a bird and colour it in yellow. I get the sticky tape and wrap it round and round the front of the jar to hold my picture in place and walk up the road two doors away to where there is a coffee shop. I'll only be gone for one song, so no one will notice me missing. I stand proudly out the front. One hand on the jar and another on my hip. I'm being brave too.

I shake and rattle the jar loudly and with my big outside voice, which is literally my inside voice too, I call out, "Donate money for the birds!"

People walk past. They ignore me. Like I'm completely not there. Like they don't see me. Maybe they can't hear me. Once again, nice and loud, "Money for the birds!"

One person walks past me and into the coffee shop and says, "No thanks." Another person says, "Don't ask me for money. I don't even like birds." Another walks past, "Go away, charity mugger!" in a meany pushy voice.

I'm nearly in tears when the coffee shop owner walks out and tells me that I can't stand there, gently nudging me away. I don't cry very often. I think crying's for babies. But this time I can't hold it back. My whole face is aching as I grit my teeth. And here come the tears. I swing around before anyone can see tears roll down my face.

I stare into the jar. My face is hot. I haven't raised one dollar for the birds. They need my help. But I have absolutely nothing and now I feel stupid. I'm not going to tell anyone about this.

I start to walk back home before anyone notices I'm gone, wishing my tears would go away. I hear a bumbling, rumbling noise from above and look up into the sky, squinting through the sun. And to my surprise, there are letters in the sky. Actual real letters.

H… O.

HO? As in Ho Ho? That's odd. We just had Christmas.

I imagine my favourite dragon from my favourite series *Yunlong and the Dragon Traders*. Yunlong lives in the clouds and rides on mist. He also breathes out clouds that can turn into rain. I think that it could be Yunlong making these letters as he speeds through the sky.

But no, it's not Yunlong, it's an aeroplane twisting and looping, letting out smoke to create another letter, P, creating H O P.

So much for a dragon! I giggle and forget about my tears. An aeroplane writing H O P in the sky is weird. The plane does another big loop and lets out more smoke.

H O P E

It then circles the word and flies out over the houses until I can't see it anymore.

Why would a plane write HOPE in the sky? What are they hoping for?

I start thinking of the birds again. I imagine that all the birds have little houses high up in the trees with food and water. There is a breeze blowing and the birds are away from the smoke. For the birds that live on the ground and can't fly, their houses sit in shrubs. These birds are busy raking the ground around their houses with their feet. I can hear the birds in the trees singing and calling to each other as they sit in the warm sunshine.

"Yo Birdie, you got them worms today?" one would call out.

"Big time!" another would call back. "Found a heap wriggling in the muddy swamp. Go before the lizards get them. Those lizards…"

I smile, the birds are happy. They are safe.

Now I'm at our front gate. I lean over the fence, open the catch and slip back inside like I was there all along. I look up at HOPE again and start to wonder.

Show and tell

Alyssa

Por Por's box lies open on Ellie's bed as I show her and Lucy the letters from Martha.

"So in this one, Martha says she's been rejected from air stewardess school," I explain. "And in this one, she's graduated and says she's trying to get a teaching job."

"Does she ever become an air stewardess?" Ellie asks.

"I can't tell. There are no more letters in the box that mention anything more about it. I know Por Por migrated to Australia with Mum in 1980 so I guess any letters would start coming to her here instead. Or they stopped writing because Por Por is here now and they just meet up or talk on the phone."

"Like us!" Ellie smiles. "Although they didn't have emails… or mobile phones… or internet."

"The handwriting is so bendy. How can you even read this, Lys?" asks Lucy.

"What's this brochure?" asks Ellie, picking up a pamphlet from the box. "It says Red Baron Flight School, premier training for your pilot needs. Get certified now!"

"Really? Show me, I saw the picture of a plane in front of the island and thought it was a holiday brochure."

"There's an address here. Let's look it up. Lys, grab my laptop on my desk?"

I get Ellie's laptop and hand it to her. She opens up the search engine and starts looking up Red Baron Flight School. Lucy and I look over her shoulder as the search items come up.

There is no Red Baron Flight School. But other flying related places come up and I point to one in the mountains very close to the address on the pamphlet.

"Ellie, click on this one. It's at Meadows Peak. It sounds so familiar. Where do I know this place? Is it near Blue Lake?"

"Sort of. It's in those mountain ranges behind Blue Lake. They're hazy and grey-blue because of the oil from the eucalyptus trees. Here." Ellie opens a new window and shows me Meadows Peak on the map.

"Have you searched up Martha?" asks Lucy.

"No, I never thought of looking her up. I've never heard Por Por mention a Martha either. I thought I knew most of her friends, there's Miriam, Goldie, Iris, then her Chinese friends, Miss Lee, Mrs Chu and Mrs Mok from the knitting crew. I didn't see an Australian lady at Por Por's memorial service, so I just assumed maybe this Martha passed away or they're no longer friends. Por Por's never mentioned her friend Martha to me. How can that be if she was such an important person in her life? I haven't brought it up with Mum either. Don't want to upset her by bringing up Por Por all the time."

"Do you want to look her up?" asks Ellie kindly.

"I guess we should."

"Okay, here goes." Ellie types Martha Goldsmith in her search engine. A bunch of Martha Goldsmiths comes up, including a lot of social media profiles, and even a few FunStar accounts!

"Martha would not have a FunStar account!" I giggle. "She can sing, *Come Fly With Me*, by Frank Sinatra! Por Por used to play this song."

"How about, *Wind Beneath my Wings*?"

"*Big Jet Plane*!" says Lucy.

"More like, Lenny Kravitz's *Fly Away*. Martha sounds… groovy – that's what old people used to say instead of cool."

"She likes the Rolling Stones," I remember. "She'd totally play a guitar and dye her hair pink like yours, Lucy."

We start giggling again. Ellie stops us when she says, "Hey, I think I found her."

She shows me a page from the annual report for Meadows Peak Aviation. There's a photo of a lady with cropped curly grey hair, standing next to a helicopter with her thumbs up. She has huge round red glasses and is wearing a boiler suit.

The caption reads, "Martha Goldsmith leads the way with charity flights across Meadows Peak. Martha is also heavily involved in our sustainability program, committed to remediation works near the non-aviation zones of our airstrip to support endangered species."

"How old is that article?" I ask Ellie.

"Only last year. Look, she has something to do with Meadows Peak Aviation, which is only a few hours away," says Ellie.

Meadows Peak Aviation's website advertises its services in scenic flights, training hours for pilots, emergency services and aerial advertising like skywriting and banners. They've got a whole section on the environment and what they're doing to support local wildlife.

"We need to get them to do the skywriting!" Lucy exclaims. "Then people will see it and help us!"

"We need to involve them in our project. Someone there will know about protecting the birds," Ellie says.

"Martha. Martha will know what to do!" I decide.

I look at Ellie. She looks at me. We're a team again!

Teen Mean

Ellie

Ding. Ding.

I warily pick up my phone. I feel the tidal wave crash onto me again.

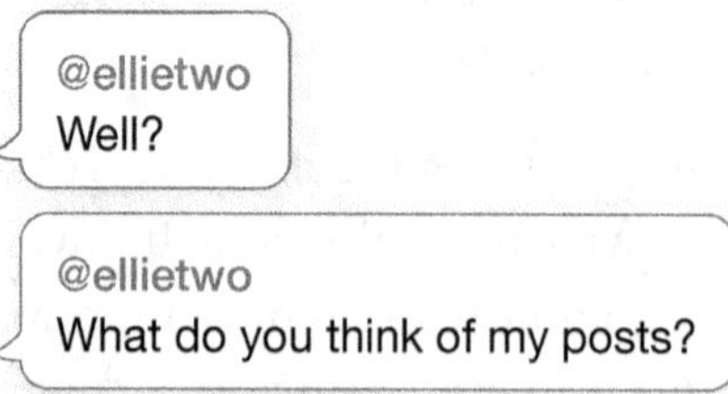

Ding. Ding. Ding.

Ding.

I shudder. I feel flushed and my heart is pounding. This shadow account following me around is scary. I wish it would go away. I'm tempted to write back but instead turn off my phone and start rummaging through my drawer. Where are those palm cards I use for debating? There they are, I grab a pencil and start drawing.

I sketch a strong dragon with a scaly spine. I close my eyes and imagine what a dragon would do in this situation. A dragon would stand up for themselves, I'm sure. They wouldn't be worried about mean words from someone hiding behind a screen. The dragon would have courage.

On another card I draw a girl sitting on a chair with flowers. She is an empress. The girl is powerful, sitting confident and composed. She doesn't look confused or irritated. I need to borrow her qualities today!

I let out a breath as I sketch a third picture. A gentle girl nurturing a flower in the palm of her hand. I imagine this nurturing girl as caring and warm. She deserves to be treated with kindness. Why would people be mean to her?

These characters are all so different. They would know what to do in this situation. Maybe I could just use their strengths for the day. That would help. I write down all the positive things they would be.

I read through all the positive qualities twice before I bundle the cards back together and put them in my bag so I have them when I need them. Which I think is going to be a lot! I shake off the thought of my shadow follower lurking somewhere ready to frighten me. I stand tall and lift my head.

The Nurturer

Warmth

Compassion

Kindness

Radiance

Gentleness

The Dragon

Renewal

Trust

Beginnings

Courage

Endurance

The Empress

Abundance

Balance

Harmony

Power

Peace

Runaway ninjas

Alyssa

This is the plan for today. Yesterday, I told Mum I'm spending the whole day with Ellie. She was ecstatic that Ellie and I made up. Ellie told her mum she's spending the whole day with me. She was ecstatic Ellie and I made up.

It's 8:30am. I pack a backpack with some snacks, sandwiches and a water bottle. My pocket money is already in my wallet in my backpack.

On my laptop, I go to the Country Trains website to double-check the timetable. It will take two hours, 26 minutes from Central Station on an express train to Meadows Peak at 10:05am.

"Bye, Mum!" I call out. "Getting the bus. Going for breakfast at Ellie's, then we're spending the day hanging, maybe the movies and general girls' stuff. Making up for lost time!"

"Okay, Lys. Love you. Say hi to Ellie for me! Text me during the day so I know you're okay!" Mum calls back from her room. She's still snoozing.

I head towards the bus stop. Bus 302 arrives on the dot at 9:18am as I expect it would. I get on and slide into the second bench behind the driver. Four stops later, a girl with yellow hair carrying a satchel bag, wearing a green cap and sunglasses gets on. She sits next to me.

"Red Parrot is on the go?" she asks.

"Affirmative," I reply.

We sit in the bus, our eyes facing forward. We are careful not to look at each other, in case we burst out laughing and drop our pretend cover.

The bus goes past some shops, the local school, the library and the park. We pass our old soccer field, its pitch more brown than green in this dry hot weather. A couple of kids are playing by the playground next to the pitch but I can't hear them laughing from inside the bus. I slide open the window and immediately smell the smoky air from the bushfires and quickly close the window again. I hope the kids are okay playing in that smoke… and the birds at Blue Lake too.

Finally, the bus arrives at the end of its route. Central Station. We get off the bus and go to the ticket booth and buy two tickets to Meadows Peak. We walk to platform six. It's 9:46am.

There's a vending machine and the girl with the yellow hair finally speaks. "Lys, they have those special edition burrito chips! I have to buy them."

"Sure. You have nineteen minutes. But I don't want to be late, so I'll give you nine minutes," I laugh.

"You want anything?"

"Actually, get me a packet. And also those Rolypolies and the Mints."

"Yep. Oh, and they have Raspberry Smashes! Two of those. Okay, that's enough. Let's go, Red Parrot."

"Affirmative."

We walk to the end of platform six and sit on the bench waiting for the train to arrive. It's 9:57am. We bought snacks in eleven minutes! Phew – good thing I gave us a buffer.

I hear the express train arrive when Ellie tugs at my sleeve.

"I'm pretty sure I just saw pink hair," Ellie whispers to me, pointing to the stairs.

I turn to look at where she's pointing but don't see anything.

"You're just nervous, Ellie. You know, lots of people have pink hair, don't they?" I reassure her.

The plan has been going so well. The train pulls up and Ellie and I walk on and sit in our designated seats. 36A and 36B. There's no one else in our carriage. All good. At 10:05am, the train pulls out of Central Station heading towards Meadows Peak.

The adventurer

Lucy

Last night I overheard Ellie on the phone to Lys when I woke up and headed to the kitchen for water.

"Uh, huh. No, I can't buy them. Mum has that app which notifies her when it's used… Yes! Bring your pocket money. Sorry, I used all mine up last week getting these cool earrings. Oh, thanks, I love them too! Yep, okay… I know, I know… that sounds fine. Second bench. Got it. What time do I need to wake up again? By 8:30am. Yep, fine… I'll tell her brekkie at yours. No, don't do that. Too risky. That's better. Uh huh. Once we're there, we can walk. It's only 30 minutes away. It'll be lunch-time and then we'll be back by six at the latest… Easy peasy apple squeezey. No idea, I just like it. Okay, bye!"

They're up to something, I knew, and I didn't want to be left out this time. I won't be left out. So I stomped back to my room. I rummaged among the pile of toys and clothes on the floor until I found my grumpy bear alarm clock.

I set it to growl and vibrate, and left it by my head so I could feel it. This morning at 8:00am, the bear's claws vibrated and he growled to wake me up. I jumped out of bed. I was already dressed in camouflage combat shorts (with pockets) and a t-shirt. I slept in them so I didn't have to bother getting dressed. Sometimes I wonder why people wear pyjamas.

I heard Ellie yell to Mum she's off trying the new breakfast place with Lys and that Lys' mum was picking her up now. Liar! I know she's probably doing something to find Martha. I can't believe they didn't include me. It's not fair. I'm the one who asked if we could look up Martha. I'm the one who wants to do the skywriting. I hate being little. It's my plan too. So I grabbed the front door before it shut and followed Ellie. I want in on the action!

Spooky Station

Alyssa

I close my eyes and take a deep breath. Oh my goodness, lying to Mum again. I can't believe I have the nerve to keep doing this. Turning off my phone makes me feel better since I can pretend I'm not lying to her.

"Ellie, I hope we're doing the right thing. It was fun to see if we could get to the train station, but now we're actually on our way, I'm freaking out!" I say.

"Lys, it'll be fine. Look we need help, don't we? A little journey and a little white lie. It's going to be okay. We'll be home once we get some answers. It's an adventure!"

Ellie decides to flip the seats in front of us over since no one's sitting there so we can put our bags in front of us and stretch out a bit. There's a newspaper on the seat facing me. "Seven-year-old missing at Demon's Gorge. Is a kidnapper on the loose?" I read. I shudder. That's awful.

Suddenly I hear a rustle behind me. We're sitting at the front of an empty carriage, so someone's come to join us. My heartbeat quickens.

"Hey..." I hear a girl's voice. It sounds a little unsure, and it sounds a little like Lucy.

I turn and sure enough, it's Lucy. Pink hair tousled. Her eyes are wide and wary. Her hands grip tightly to the back of the seats behind us.

"Lucy!" Ellie says in shock. "Oh my gosh. Lucy! I can't believe it. What are you doing here?"

"Lucy! Did you follow us? Are you okay?"

Ellie stares at her, still in shock.

"I'm sorry. I'm sorry…" Lucy speaks up. "I didn't know. I followed you out of the house. I sneaked onto the bus from the back door, dodging behind a guy who was getting off. Then I just jumped onto the train after you. And now… and now I need you to know I'm here. I miss Mum, I'm hungry, I'm…"

She trails off. She starts picking a hole in the plastic on the headrest in front of her. Pick, pick, pick.

"Lucy, stop doing that. Sit down here in front of us." I push away the newspaper, flipping the scary article face down.

Ellie slumps down in her seat and sighs. She says, "I knew it was all going too well." She takes her phone out. "Maybe we should call Mum now. We'll get off at the next station and turn around. I'm totally going to get grounded. Mum will blame me for sure. It's going to be a long grounding – weeks, months even. Oh gosh, I might have to miss the Icebreaker Dance at school… Lucy, what did you even tell Mum?"

"I left a note that Aunty Jam picked me up and took me to the movies," Lucy whispers, looking down.

"And you think Mum would believe that? She would ring Aunty Jam for sure. Oh my gosh, she's probably called the police by now. I'm just going to text her now and tell her Aunty Jam caught up with us at brekkie and we're all at the movies together…"

"Ellie, that's a good plan for now. But what are we doing… more lies. Oh gosh. Okay, once we get back onto the return train, we'll know a time and we can tell our parents when we'll be home and everyone will be less worried," I suggest.

"What did I do without you for six months?" Ellie asks. "Okay – let's get off at the next stop. We can still use these return tickets, right?"

Just then the train slows down and rolls to a stop at a station. We grab our things and get off the train. We are the only people who get off. The train door shuts quickly behind us and the train speeds off like it found the place creepy.

This station is deserted. There's peeling paint on the single bench and a rickety shed where a small shop used to be, selling newspapers or small snacks to passengers.

Once the train is gone, it's silent. I can hear us breathing, it's that quiet. Ellie and I look at each other.

"Let's quickly look up the next train back to Central," Ellie says.

I turn my phone back on. Phew, nothing from Mum.

"I have bad reception on my phone… is there a station person we can ask?" says Ellie.

"This shed is probably where they would be. But it's shut." I look around and notice bright orange and white barricades set up across part of the station, blocking a flight of stairs that lead down under the train tracks. A small worksite is set up by the stairs, bordered off from passengers with a makeshift gate, some orange safety cones, helmets, warning signs and tools. "Platform closed. Do not enter" a sign reads.

"Look, this poster could be a timetable. Gee, it's hard to read – the glass is so dirty and scratched and what's with this graffiti? Dogs or cats?"

"Dogs, of course," answers Lucy.

"Shush, Lucy. That wasn't a question for you, durrr. Lys was just reading the graffiti," says Ellie with her hands on her hips.

"Come on, you two. I hope this is correct. Weekend timetable, then it's got the time here…"

"Lys, Lys… over there!" Ellie whispers. She points over to where the gate is. "It moved!"

"What do you mean it moved? It's just some rubbish, isn't it? A pile of rags… oh my goodness… you're right, it moved! What the heck? It's just the wind…" My voice shakes a little.

But there's no wind. The air is hot and dry. I see the lump shift again and then I see a mound protrude upwards.

"Ellie, I think it's a person! Maybe it's a dog? Dog or cat?"

"Or… what if it's the kidnapper guy? Yeah, I saw the newspaper article too…"

"Ellie, that's just your imagination. Could be a homeless person. I saw heaps in Hong Kong, really sad…"

"But what if it's the kidnapper? The person who kidnapped that seven-year-old? When is the next train out of here?"

"Okay, okay – here it says the next train back to Central is at 12:08pm." I say, "Oh wow, it's an hour away. Lucy, sit here and we'll wait."

We sit down on the bench and keep a sharp eye on the kidnapper lump mound thing. We bring out sandwiches we'd packed and share them for lunch. 15 minutes pass… 20 minutes pass. I glance over at the lump.

I hear a rustle coming from behind me. I hear it again, louder this time so I turn towards the kidnapper mound instinctively. At the same time Lucy tugs at my sleeve and points at the mound.

"Oh no," I mouth silently as I turn towards Ellie. Her eyes widen.

"We're going to die here," she whispers dramatically. Her hands grasp at my other arm.

"Ellie, don't be silly. It's going to be cool…" I reassure her but not really believing my words.

Lucy stands up and peers over at the shifting lump.

"Lucy!" Ellie and I both squeal. I grab her shoulder.

"Sit down!"

"You'll get us killed."

"I think we should run!"

"Grab our stuff. Quickly!"

I see the lump wriggling about, left and right. It looks agitated. The rags covering it start lifting upwards and separate into two distinct parts, a smaller head-like lump at the top and a bigger body in the middle. The head lump lifts up, like it's surveying the scene. Looking for something. Us!

Lucy stands her ground and shakes off my hands on her shoulder. She looks annoyed. Like the lump's making her bad day even worse. She takes her half-eaten cheese sandwich and throws it at the lump.

"Go away!" she shouts at it.

The cheese sandwich breaks apart mid-air. Almost as if in slow motion, the cheese flops onto the ground. One piece of bread hits the head-like lump with a plop and ricochets about half a metre away from the pile of rags. The head shakes and a furry paw peeps out from under the rags to scratch at its head. The scratching moves the rags away and out pops a cute tabby cat. The cat raises its head, finds the two separated pieces of bread on the ground and goes to pick up the discarded cheese. It looks over at us curiously, sensing the source of the sandwich, but clearly hunger takes over and the cat pads away with the sandwich pieces in its mouth and wriggles into a sunny spot behind the makeshift gates. It lies down and starts eating Lucy's cheese sandwich.

We each sit back down on the bench and stare shell-shocked at the empty train tracks. Finally, I say, "So the answer is cat…"

We burst out laughing, giddy with relief and the realisation of just how silly we were. After we calm down, I look at my phone again and think about what my next lie to Mum is going to be. I can't believe I've becoming a lying-to-Mum kind of person!

"Lys," Ellie says softly, when she sees me on the phone again. "Are we doing the right thing? Look, I know we should maybe head back…" She glances over at Lucy who's wandered over to the sunny spot behind the makeshift gate to look at the cat.

"Oh gosh, Lucy, can you not wander off like that? Make sure we can still see you! Do not touch the cat!" She turns back to me. "I cannot believe her. She's so… so… crazy sometimes. Who wanders off to look at a random cat?"

"What did you mean just then when you asked if we're doing the right thing? Lucy's run away and she's little. Sure, she just saved us from a menacing cat, but it's not responsible to go all the way to Meadows Peak with her. We need to take her home."

"You know, it's only half an hour away. I'll text Mum that we're going to your place after the movie and get Aunty Jam to cover for us. Here…" she starts reading as she's texting, "Aunty Jam, we took Lucy to see *Dragon Warrior 2*, it's PG so Mum needs to know you're with us – cover for us pleeeassee!"

Ellie grins. "Oh, she's writing back straight away. Yes! She said yes!

"You know, Lys, we left pretty early, we can still catch the next train to Meadows Peak, talk to the Aviation place about wildlife protection, find out if Martha is there and still get home. We've forgotten our purpose which was to involve them in our project. We can't give up now. We just can't."

"Ellie, I hope you know what you're doing," I say to her. "Because I trust you. If you believe this will work, then I do too. And you're right, we're already in this mess. Another hour at the movies isn't so bad, is it?"

I hope I sound more confident than I feel. I look at the mountains and think of Martha's adventurer girl climbing upwards. I try to borrow a bit of that courage.

Decisions

Ellie

"Lucy, Lucy, hurrrryyyy!"

"Come on, Lucy – quickly!"

"The train's here!"

"Come on!!!"

I can hear the squeal of the train on the tracks and the metallic sounds from afar getting closer. The train is approaching and Lucy is moving at the slowest speed possible.

She screams, "The gate! The gate's stuck! I can't move it! Help! Ellie! Lys!"

There are two trains approaching, and they're coming from either side of the platform. One train heads back home to Central and the other one onwards to Meadows Peak. One back to not getting into more trouble and one to seeing what lies ahead.

I look at Lys and she looks at me. She nods. I run towards the makeshift gate by the stairs and see Lucy on the stair behind the gate trying to get out. I don't have time to think what craziness that cat's been subjected to as I yank as hard as I can on the gate. It shifts with just enough of a gap to squeeze Lucy through and haul her towards me. I lift her up like a giant soccer ball and run as fast as I can back towards Lys. We haven't actually said anything aloud on what we want to do next. Decisions are hard to make.

Lys grabs all our bags. Two backpacks hanging off one narrow shoulder, my satchel on the crook of her free arm. Her face looks determined, but she's smiling. Ever so slightly, she crooks her head towards one side.

Together we leap onto the train as the door shuts. The closing door knocks into one of the backpacks, unbalancing Lys. Lucy slides down my hip as I grab at Lys' shoulder to steady her.

We've made the same decision – the one heading towards Meadows Peak. The one heading to a new adventure.

Sunday rest day

Alyssa

Lucy, Ellie and I get out of Meadows Peak train station and cross the main road. Compared to that old train station, this is much better! There's a small cafe next to the station, with green potted plants lining its patio. An older couple sit there having their lunch. There's a newsagent and a bakery, as well as the Post Office with a sign, Meadows Peak, Population 112. I see a few people walking around. The air is still warm and dry and a little bit smoky. Outside the newsagent is a stand for the front of a magazine. "Birds Ablaze!" it reads.

My eyes widen at that headline. I hope the birds are not actually on fire! I feel determined again.

Ellie holds Lucy's hand as we check in with a passerby that we're walking down Lorikeet Road and that it will take us to Meadows Peak Aviation. We're on the right track!

We walk silently for several minutes taking in the tall gum trees that line the road. Lucy and Ellie walk hand in hand in front of me. The gum trees here are tall and narrow, not the gnarly type that I'm used to. They grow tightly together and shoot upwards like soldiers protecting their land. Strips of rough dark brown bark fall down their trunks like ribbons, revealing the smooth light grey trunk underneath. The light grey trunk is on the top half of the tree, and the brown ribbons curl on the bottom half. I have never seen this type of gum tree before, with the curly brown bark ribbons that have fallen off the trees resting on the ground pooling around our feet. We walk on the soft bark. I pretend it's a brown "red carpet" leading us to a magical fortress where we've been invited to help the kingdom in their plight against evil invaders. Our tall tree soldiers are our friends, providing guidance, their branches pointing the way towards the fortress. In a way, that's what we hope to do.

After twenty minutes or so, Lucy says she's tired and her throat is dry. We stop and sit on a fallen log to drink some water. We'd refilled our water bottles at the station. The sun is high in the sky and it's hot and smoky. Our faces are red and sweaty. We're puffed out.

"How much longer do we have to walk?" asks Lucy.

"I would say another fifteen minutes. You're doing so well!" says Ellie.

"I'm sorry…" Lucy says in a solemn voice that I've never heard before.

"Why?" I ask.

"That I followed you. I'm sorry to get you into this trouble. If I weren't here you would have arrived earlier, it would be quicker to walk and you wouldn't have to stop and rest."

"Lucy, it's okay. We didn't include you in our plans and that wasn't right either," Ellie says.

"We forget how quickly you've grown up, too," I add.

"Besides we're happy you got to see these tall gum trees with the falling bark with us! I don't think I could have described them very well to you if you didn't see them with your own eyes!" Ellie says.

"I like them. It's like they're wearing brown floaty skirts with a light-coloured top!" Lucy replies.

With that, we laugh. "I was thinking they look like soldiers!" I tell them.

"You can be a soldier and still wear a brown floaty skirt."

"True."

Ellie pulls out her phone. "Better text Mum."

Once we're done texting, Ellie says, "Let's walk now – a bit slower and we'll get there before we know it. Just one step at a time."

We continue our journey marvelling at our soldier friends and their floaty skirts. We start naming them as we walk along, pretending they're talking to each other.

"Hello Gretel, I love your dress!" we call out.

"Thank you, Louise. My my, that brown skirt matches your brown top!"

"You are too kind, Crystal. I borrowed this skirt from Dana over there."

"That Dana, she's so kind. She has a nice brown dress on, too. Her's is more chocolatey brown. Do you like my green hat and matching leafy gloves?"

"Brown is the latest colour all the ladies are wearing around these parts. But what about our gentlemen friends?"

"Robert also likes to wear a lot of brown. He prefers the light brown look with the rusty brown floaty pants. He is partial to little yellow flowers too."

"How interesting, so does Monty. In fact, all the male trees like the brown look too. We're all wearing brown floaty bottoms these days with green hats!" We all laugh.

Before we know it, we've reached the end of the road. There's a medium-sized tin shed in a cleared part of the bushland, and behind it a vast paddock for the airfield. There's a couple of small planes with the propeller on their noses and one helicopter. A small sign announces, "Meadows Peak Aviation. Welcome!"

We squeal with excitement and run towards the tin shed. We run up the pathway and climb a few steps up a porch to get to the front door. It's shut.

I peer inside and no one's there. There's an office desk, an area with pamphlets and posters on the walls, and some stools by the wall where you can wait, presumably for your flight. There's a water cooler and some plants. The lights are off.

Ellie knocks on the door, but clearly no one's home. We walk around the building and peer into a side window that looks into a little office. Again, it's empty. The computer is turned off and there's no one behind the desk. We walk to the back where it leads to the airfield and there's a gate. It says: "No entry. Authorised persons only." A stick figure is drawn on the sign with a red circle and a huge X marked across the figure. So rude. Not only does it say no entry but they have to rub it in with a big giant red cross! There's a heavy chain and huge padlock on the gate too.

I sigh loudly. We planned so much, we looked up everything, we tried very hard to get here and even had a few detours, and finally we're here and the place is shut.

"Ellie, Lucy, I'm so sorry. This is all my fault. I feel so stupid. We should never have come here. What a waste of time," I say sadly. "We should have called up and checked."

"I'm sure there's something we can do. Let me find a number to call."

"It's no use. It's closed for today. Of all the things we checked, we didn't check the opening hours."

"It's my fault then. You would have gotten here earlier if I wasn't here," says Lucy.

"No, I shouldn't have gotten so mad and made us turn around. If we kept going, we would be fine," Ellie insists.

"Maybe it never opened on a Sunday. I just assumed it would be open because of the scenic flights. You'd think people would want to fly on the weekends."

I look up at the mountains above us, majestic and immovable. They're not going anywhere. I take a deep breath. It would be lovely if the air wasn't thick with smoke. We walk back around to the front of the shed and I sit down on the steps. Ellie and Lucy join me, sitting close together. We lean against each other. I put my head on Ellie's shoulder and sigh. "Oh well, we tried. It'll be here another day. At least we found it."

Ellie puts one arm across my shoulders and gives me a little squeeze. "Let's sit here and rest up a bit before we head back."

Hope

Ellie

Poor Lys. She really hoped we'd find someone to help us with our quest for the birds at Blue Lake. We all did. We sit together for some time. There is nothing to say.

My phone vibrates. Mum asks whether we'll have dinner with Lys and I think about what I should text back. Among all my worries I also think we need to get back to the train station soon and not miss the last train home. It would be awful to stuff that up too.

The distant sound of a truck on the gravel road startles us. It had been so quiet and we hadn't come across any cars on our walk here that we're surprised by the mechanical noise. All we've been hearing in the past hour are the soft leaves rustling and cicadas. The truck is coming towards us as the sound of the engine and wheels on the gravel gradually gets louder. We all glance at each other. I think we are all thinking the same thing – is it the kidnapper? The truck parks about 50 metres away from us and a lady gets out. She winces a little when she hops out of the truck but she approaches us with briskness.

"Oi, you three youngsters! Saw you on the security camera sneaking about. Lucky I live down the road. That's why we put those locks on – are you the ones who have been putting graffiti on our walls? I personally like some organic artwork myself and admire graffiti artists, but to be honest, the stuff you kids have been spraying on our walls, well no offence but that's not art. Just messy scribbles. Now why are you here? We had to close on Sundays because of my hip. Where are your adults? Don't just…"

She stops speaking when she gets close to us.

Lys and I are standing now and walk down the steps to meet her. I ask Lucy to stay on the steps and rest while we sort this out.

When the lady stops, she stares at Lys. A pair of large red glasses is tucked up in her hair. She has bushy grey hair. She pulls the glasses down onto her nose and stares at Lys some more.

"Oh my," she says breathlessly. "I feel like I've travelled back in time."

Cookies and cream

Lucy

I'm tired and hungry. I lean against the railing of the steps I'm sitting on, while Ellie and Lys talk to the lady. She looks like she is 120 years old.

Actually, why sit up when you can rest your head? I put my head down on a higher step. It's been such a long hot day. All this walking. Should have brought my scooter! My legs are heavy. My arms feel heavy and my eyes are heavy. I close my eyes for a little rest. I start thinking about the birds again. I imagine them happy in the trees. They're singing to each other in my mind. I feel myself falling asleep and force myself to wake up. Come on, Lucy!

Ellie and Lys are still deep in conversation with the lady. Looks serious. Every now and then they glance my way. I shove my hands in my pocket and feel something cookie-like. It is a cookie! I break a small piece off. It's the best – all chocolatey, sweet and yummy. I gobble it all down.

Martha

Alyssa

I stare back at the lady. She's still looking at me as she rubs her eyes under her glasses.

"Get a grip, Goldie," she says. "Don't scare them with your sentimentality. Hello, don't mind me. Now let's start again. What are you young ladies doing here at Meadows Peak Aviation?"

"Umm," I start to speak. She looks like she could be the Martha in the Meadows Peak Aviation website photo, but she's just called herself Goldie? Por Por's friend who couldn't come to Hong Kong? I smack my forehead with my palm. Martha Goldsmith. Goldie.

Ellie takes over, "We're looking for someone to help us. I'm Ellie, this is my friend Alyssa and my sister over there is Lucy. We haven't done anything wrong – well, we've lied to our mums, told them we're at the movies instead of coming here all by ourselves, but we totally have not done anything wrong to you. We haven't tried to open the door or steal anything. We didn't do any of the graffiti, I promise. We're just on a bit of a mission and we saw on your website that you have a program that saves local birds and we wondered if we could be part of that."

"I'm sorry we bothered you and you had to come get us," I finally manage to add. "But we really need some help. You see, we thought we could help the birds at Blue Lake. They're flying away, probably from the bushfires and staying in Ellie's backyard! Lucy there made them a birdhouse. So we thought we could do more to help them, but nothing seems to work."

"We did a petition and wrote to the Mayor of Blue Lake, that didn't work."

"We tried to raise some money."

"That was a total fail."

"We thought you might be able to help with your conservation work and…"

"Skywriting!" calls Lucy dreamily from the steps.

"Can you help?" I ask softly.

"Sure I can," Martha nods. "Been helping your family for over 50 years now, haven't I?" Then she smiles. "First of all, how about I call your mum?"

She winks at me, walks back to her car and takes out a giant phone. It's an old mobile phone, which looks like a brick. She explains, "Never got around to upgrading and besides this one works fine." It looks like she's seriously had this phone since 1997.

Ellie and I are glued to our spots. I'm sure my mouth is open but I don't know what to say. She's going to get us in trouble with Mum. Lucy looks like she's fallen asleep on the steps.

"Madeline sweetie, it's Martha. How are you? I heard from Lily the service went well and you only argued about the duck like a hundred times! You know to let Lily cook it her way even though your mum loved it smoked… I know you made it for Mei, but I've learnt never to argue with Lily in the kitchen." Martha speaks loudly into the phone, like she's worried Mum won't hear her.

"My hip is fine, dear – doctor says I'm good to go now. Damn hips, you can't do anything about them much at my age." She waves her hands around wildly as she explains.

"So I'm calling to let you know something interesting. Lyssie's here with me. She's fine, she's fine. Actually, never better! I forget how quickly they can grow up on you when you're not watching! She's a bit confused though – think Mei calling me Goldie all these years because of that one time in the eighties I dyed my hair blonde (bad mistake!) is confusing her as much as it confuses the heck out of everyone else! Makes me sad that I've been flying about and so busy with my conservation work in the last few years and not seen her or you recently. But here she is. She's with her friends Ellie and Lucy. It was my idea to see her out of the blue. I miss Mei. A lot. My idea about the movies. Sorry if it's a shock, but you know me. Not one to let things just happen. Go hard or go home, I say. It's getting into the afternoon though and I'd like to spend more time with them. Such funny ducklings, these three. Who would've thought I'd like children!"

She smirks at us when she said that last bit.

"I'll get them home to you first thing in the morning, if that's okay with you? They can stay the night with me. It's no trouble. Can you call Ellie and Lucy's mum, too? Just tell her I offered some help. She knows me well enough now too since you ladies made those cupcakes for our fundraiser early last year. Great, that's settled then!"

Alyssa's journal

Today I am grateful for...

- The strength of friendship. Martha knows me!
  She's the one Por Por calls Goldie. She's known
  me all my life and received updates from Por Por
  all the time. And for Ellie taking this trip with
  me and helping me.

- Martha not telling Mum the whole truth.

- A warm and safe place to stay. I feel like one
  of those little birds in Ellie and Lucy's backyard...
  a little bird who flew away from her home and
  now has a safe place to stay.

Quote of the day

"Hope is the thing with feathers
That perches in the soul
And sings the tune without the words
And never stops at all."

Emily Dickinson

Old times

Ellie

Over pizzas we talk to Martha about her life at Meadows Peak now and how much she loves it in the mountains. We tell her about Blue Lake and how sad we feel about the wildlife and their burnt homes.

She knew all about Blue Lake of course, being so close to it. There are 94 bird species in the Meadows Peak area and she shows us her bird-watching journal where she has personally catalogued 38 birds. I love her bird sketches and photos. There are some feathers she has picked up and we read her descriptions of the birdsongs.

At Meadows Peak Aviation, she's in charge of all the environmental issues they face. It sounds like a big job. Martha stands up from the dining table to go over to her little study area to grab something to show us.

"You know, when I was young and moved into the area, all I cared about was the flying," she tells us. She turns to look at us. "But then I realised how much damage the airfield was causing to the neighbours with our noise, and to the trees with our pollution and to the animals. That's when I decided we needed to change. No one else was going to do it, so I did."

"What did you do?" Lys asked.

"Well, aircrafts have an impact on bird populations. We have lots of honeyeaters around these parts, cockatoos and lyrebirds. Ah, here's what I was looking for."

Lys and I look at each other when she mentions the lyrebirds. Martha returns to the dining table with a stack of paper clipped together with a bulldog clip.

"You've heard of the lyrebirds, girls? Beautiful birds with a beautiful song. But the aircraft noise upsets the lyrebirds because they call to each other so much, you know, about food or warnings and even for mating. I'm sorry to tell you, sometimes birds get injured by the aircrafts and even the force of the wind a helicopter creates can be very harmful to the little ones."

Martha unclips her stack of paper and lays the sheets out next to the plate of pizza crusts.

"We have a tonne of different plants around here. Did you see them on your walk? You must come back in autumn, when the banksias are in full bloom. It's gorgeous and full of nectar, which the honeyeaters just love.

"Last year we did some research on the honeyeaters in the area. It took me a long time to get the company to agree to reduce flights in autumn. We make less money for sure, but you can't injure those lovely birds."

"But if you make less money, will you have to close?" Lys asks, worried.

"So if you're smart," Martha says as she points to a section in her plan, "you can ask the government to help you out financially. I spent a long time researching the honeyeaters to prove how many more we get in the autumn months."

We marvel at her plan and Lys takes a closer look at the research section on the honeyeaters.

Through all this time, Lucy's been pretty quiet. I glance over at her sitting at the head of the dining table. I notice her eyes drooping shut and her head starting to wobble as she struggles to keep up with the conversation. She can't fight it anymore.

Martha grabs a colourful crochet blanket from her sofa and wraps it over Lucy's shoulders. The clashing colours on the crochet blanket against Lucy's pink hair make me smile. Blue against pink against orange with purple pom poms.

"Come on, Lucy, let me tell you a bedtime story about a singing firefighter. Maybe it's bedtime for everyone, girls. We can pick up the conversation tomorrow," Martha says as she leads Lucy to her bedroom.

Martha's voice is soft as she reads to Lucy. "The hot air came first. Then came the smell. Burning smells replaced the soft freshness of the eucalyptus leaves. The air was thick and heavy. Then the sky turned black." Martha pauses dramatically before continuing. "Lottie shook her head. She flapped her wings around her face to wave the smoke away..." In my mind I picture a golden wing waving away the smoke. I turn to tell Lys but I stop to admire a second crazy colourful crochet blanket on the sofa. This one has an intricate flower pattern that spirals outwards.

I have a very similar one in my bedroom. Lys's Por Por gave it to me for Christmas one year.

"That blanket looks familiar!" I say to Lys.

She laughs. "Por Por made so many of those blankets to sell that time her knitting crew was trying to raise money for their friend's medical bills. Looks like Martha bought a couple!"

We spread the crochet blanket out over the sofa so we can follow the colours of the spiralling flowers.

"Why do you think Por Por loved making all her knitted things so much?" I ask.

"I guess it was a way for her to be creative. She worked at the clothing factory so she must have picked up some love for making things from there."

"We don't make nearly enough things, do we? Did she ever teach you?"

"She tried. But I wasn't interested. I feel bad about that now."

"Oh, don't be. I bet she loved seeing you wear everything she made for you."

Lys gives me a look.

"Sure, that one time the pink and red jumper with the strawberries was way out there and you cried because you didn't like it but had to wear it anyway. I reckon you would totally wear it now! In fact it's quite trendy, loud jumpers, with fruit on them. Would totally brighten up a FunStar video," I laugh.

"I know. Look at these patterns. Wow, that's something isn't it?"

I trace a pink flower with my finger, following the curvy lines this way and that. Lys traces a blue flower with hers. We each follow the threads of our flowers until our fingers meet in the middle to find a giant crochet strawberry. We hook our fingers together in a little finger shake and giggle.

Sleepover

Alyssa

I'm on the foldout bed in the living-room. Ellie and Lucy are in Martha's room sharing her bed. Martha says because of her back she much prefers the foldout mattress on the floor of her little study anyway. The lights are off and we're all trying to rest after today's crazy day.

Martha pops her head out of the study and calls out softly, "Coo-ee, Alyssa. You still awake?"

"Yes, sort of," I say sleepily.

"Okay, I found something for you, which I was going to mail to your mum. But since you're here, I'll give them to you now."

"What is it?" I say as I prop myself up on my elbows.

She walks out of her room in a pair of baggy brown pyjamas. "These are the business class Air Australia pyjamas back in the day when they used to give them to long haul passengers. Do you like them? I got them off the internet. Could never afford to fly business class myself!

"Here you go." She hands over a rolled-up bunch of rumpled papers to me. "These are for you."

I look at the papers in my hand. There are about a dozen envelopes all addressed to Martha in small neat handwriting. The top one has a stamp with the profile of Queen Elizabeth II and Hong Kong written beneath. The date stamped across it is 21 June 1968. They're the return letters!

I sit up and Martha turns on the lamp beside the sofa. She grins and it feels like I'm with Por Por. I start to say thank you, but she beats me to it and says, "Shh, I'll leave you two together." She pats my head and shuffles back to the study.

I fall asleep as I read the letters, Por Por by my side.

Mei-Lan Lee
Flat 17, Block 9 Community Flats
1827 Orchard Terrace
Kowloon, Hong Kong

21 June 1968

Martha Goldsmith
9 Sandyview Street
Quiet Meadows, Australia

Dear Martha,

I hope you had a safe journey back to Australia. Please do tell me what flying on an aeroplane is like – I cannot imagine being thousands of feet high in the sky, seeing the small people down below.

Do you fly next to the birds? What happens when the clouds come into the room? Was it as wonderful as we saw on the news on television? Do you have a television at home? I really hope you do, so you can tell me what you have been watching, because no one I know owns a television here. When I make enough money, I will buy one for my family.

The last time I watched a television was in the classroom with you two months ago. That feels like a long time ago and I have many things to tell you already. Do you remember sitting in the hot classroom, on those hard wooden benches, leaning as far forward as we could, to see the screen? I remember Jin shoving me with his pointy elbows, his smelly breath down my neck and then you pretending to kick his bag across the room by mistake, so he had to get up to retrieve it. Oh my, the look he had on his face!

Your father was the kindest teacher at our school. He would run those after school News Broadcasting classes and let us sit so close to the television and turn the dial to find the right spot so we could watch the news, but then secretly allow us to watch 'Doctor Who' which came on straight afterwards. It was such a treat! Each week, we were so worried we would miss an episode — it was on at 5:15pm. I wish I had a TARDIS, like Doctor Who so I could travel back in time to see you again!

How is your father going at his new school in Australia? How is the teaching college you are attending? I am still sad sometimes thinking about your family moving back to Australia and that for me, school has finished forever. It still does not feel real to wake up and not put on my school dress and find you sitting under the tree by the front gate to go to our first lesson together. When you moved to Hong Kong to be in my class after your father transferred to our school to teach us English — this was truly the most wonderful thing to happen to me (well, just as important as getting my scholarship, otherwise we would never have become friends). In the past six years, you taught me so much about the greater world and I learnt to speak and write in English.

My mother and father still think I am making my
English up! My brother makes fun of me reading
the books you left for me all the time. He calls me
Little Miss Uppity (in Chinese). I ignore him. What
a bore. He should do something to improve himself.
I offered to teach him but he doesn't want to
learn. He asks why do I want to turn him into an
Englishman, a foreigner, something he's not. That's
not what I mean at all. I don't understand him.

I got a job at the garment factory! It is the oldest
but most respected factory in Hong Kong. It takes
an hour and a half to get there, so I need to wake
up at 6am, make breakfast for Lily and Ann, take
them to the school bus and then I walk down to
the bus that takes me to the ferry wharf, and then
I catch the ferry to town and walk 15 minutes to
the factory by 8:30am.

My job is to count the rolls of cloth that come from
the truck and into the storeroom. I count them
when they are in the storeroom and write them
down in a notebook and tally them each day.
I count them again at the end of the day. Then
I give the report to Mr Mouse, the factory manager.

The factory manager is a small, quiet man. He
doesn't talk much and when I hand him the report
at the end of the day, he looks at me nervously,
twitches his head, takes the report and scurries
away. He actually scurries and twitches, like a
little mouse – I have never seen him walk or stride
or march. This is why everyone at the factory calls

him Mr Mouse. At first I thought how apt that he is called Mr Mouse because he acts like a mouse. Turns out this is what people have called him all his life. No one even remembers his real name.

There is a bigger boss, Mr Davenport. Yes, he is English. But his family has been in Hong Kong since the 1850s when the English first arrived! Can you imagine the 1850s – what life must have been like then compared to now. It must have been awful without flushing toilets! I mention it because you were shocked at my flat where we share the "outhouse" as you call it, with our neighbours, but at least it flushes. Imagine one where you have to bring in the water – or take out the bucket of waste – or empty the bucket or whatever you have to do. Sorry, this is an awful topic to end on. "So unladylike!" as Principal Watson would say in her fake British accent.

I wish I could come and visit you one day in Australia. Please write back to me as I am eager to hear about your new life. I wish I could continue my education like you can, but life here is good enough. I make $5 a day. It is not a lot but I imagine it is what a new starter can make. I am grateful I got a job straightaway and it is in the good part of the factory too! I work with other women doing the paperwork. I am lucky that because of the scholarship I can read and write and count. I know it won't be long before I need to get married – you know it's only two years until we're 20. So I'm making the most of it, which is something you say a lot! I still don't really know exactly what I am supposed to make the most of!

In the lunchroom, I sometimes look around to see if any of the boys are worth talking to – no one has caught my eye. It's such a drag thinking about boys. I'd rather talk about those horses at your uncle's farm.

Your true friend,

Mei

Mei-Lan Lee
Flat 17, Block 9 Community Flats
1827 Orchard Terrace
Kowloon, Hong Kong

21 February 1969

Martha Goldsmith
9 Sandyview Street
Quiet Meadows, Australia

Dear Martha,

It takes so long to get a letter from you and for you to receive mine that so many things have happened in the middle. We just had a wonderful Chinese new year! Imagine if one day in the year 2000, we can talk to each other as if we were face to face — me sitting on the lower bunk bed in my little room with the noisy cars honking outside and you in that "backyard" you talk about with birds singing in the blue bum trees. Then you say to me, "GUM not BUM!"

Ha — that blows my mind!

I cannot think of anyone more suited to a life of adventure FLYING than you. To me, you've always been like you are FLYING. Whooshing in with your ideas, getting us into trouble. Also, it was your grand idea to help me with my English when you moved to Hong Kong to be in my class after your father transferred to our school.

If you think being an air stewardess will give you that feeling of joy, then go for it!

I want to tell you a secret. Something is going down at the factory. Last month Wai Ming, who is in charge of the workers' pay at the factory, had to go back to his village unexpectedly, so Mr Mouse asked me to do Wai Ming's tasks, counting the hours people work and making sure they get paid every week.

At first I was honoured he'd asked me! A girl who's only worked for half a year, who barely knows her way around the factory. I still get lost on the old factory floor.

One day I was in a toilet stall, when I overheard a lady complain to her friend that she doesn't get paid as much as some guy called Bo Beng in her button sewing team because she saw Bo Beng's wife at the market on the weekend buying oranges, and who can afford oranges when there is a shortage of fresh fruit at the moment?

She was so furious because she and Bo Beng do the exact same work and started on the exact same day. They both sew buttons onto shirts and have been doing it for five years now — she even said she does it better than him! Well I can't be the judge of that, but it did make me curious. And very upset for her if this were true.

The next time I had the salary book I was curious. I didn't know Toilet Button Lady's name, so I couldn't look her up, but I found Bo Beng and he gets $8 for each hour he works. I looked for all the people who sew buttons. It was true! Some people get $5 and some get $8. Toilet Button Lady must only get $5 because I saw a lot of women's names getting $5 an hour. Why was there a difference if they started at the same time and do the exact same job?

I thought to myself, this doesn't seem fair. But I am just a young girl who has newly started. I don't want to cause a scene. Although Toilet Button Lady seemed so upset. And her friend was also very upset about it too. For five years, working so hard and still only getting paid the same $5 an hour.

The next time I saw Mr Mouse, I decided to ask him, "Mr Mouse, why do some people get different pay? I just want to make sure I get my maths right. I would hate to make a mistake."

He twitched and rubbed his nose a bit with the back of his hands. He glanced about. Then he pulled me aside and explained in a whisper, "Yes, some people get paid differently. You see some families have worked for this factory for a very long time, usually the men, and we reward them for that. They have been here a long time and we know they will be here a long time. So they get more. But the women don't stay as long. We try to look after everyone here." He then looked up at me for the first time ever. "It is how things are, Mei-Lan."

As he turned around to scurry away, I was thinking, hang on, but they do the same job. That's not right.

"Um, Mr Mouse!" I called after him.

He turned around and looked up at me very briefly, then back at the floor. He didn't walk away so I kept going. "I guess that might make sense to you. But even if they do the same job? Maybe if they have been here longer, they should get more pay only if they do something more difficult...?"

He sighed and said to the floor, "Mei-Lan, you are young and you will learn soon, but some things are better left the way they are. You can't change the things you can't change. Mei-Lan, 'A bird can roost but on one branch, a mouse can drink not more than its fill from the river.'"

So he recites a famous Chinese proverb. At first, I thought it was silly using a saying about a mouse given his nickname is Mr Mouse. But I started to think about it. It means you have enough and don't need anything more. Well, I'm not sure that's fair. Toilet Button Lady might not feel that way on less money than the person standing next to her doing the same thing. It's more about what's fair than what's enough.

I don't know, Martha, but I really feel sad for Toilet Button Lady and her friend. Sad isn't even the word. I have a word in Chinese which I don't have in English. It's like my inside is moving around and I am angry and I want to shout at someone.

People want to do their job and they can't help it if they've got to leave the job later. You do your job well, you do it the same as everyone else, you should be paid the same. Also, it just sounds like an excuse to say it's for loyalty. I'm not born into the right family so will I ever get very far? I think it's because they just want to pay women less. That just makes me feel more of the crazy shouting kind of angry. I had to do some of that breathing you told me about.

What would someone clever like you say to me? I could really use your advice right now. In particular, about the shouting kind of angry which I don't have an English word for.

Your friend,

Mei

Breakfast buffet

Lucy

I wake up to my tummy growling out loud. I'm starving. I tiptoe to the kitchen so I don't wake anyone up but Ellie and Alyssa are already there. They're standing at the fridge with the doors wide open. Looks like we're all hungry!

"Sis, can you get me something to eat?" I say.

"I don't know what to eat!"

I duck under Ellie's arm to see inside and I see what she means. There are lots of jars and bowls inside but all the food is different to what we have at home.

"Els, let's do a buffet like when we go on holidays," I say.

I grab some cheese and hand it over to Lys. She sniffs it, shrugs and places it onto the table. Ellie finds a jar with an assortment of biscuits and crackers inside. She searches around and manages to find enough plain crackers and puts them on a dinner plate.

I try to look inside the jars – jam, olives, cucumbers, cabbages in chilli, and peanut butter. Crunchy – cool, much better than smooth. I take out the peanut butter. I see a chocolate bar and grab that, too!

Better have something healthy to balance the chocolate. I find some grapes and toss them onto the table. There's carrot cake, already sliced. That's not too bad. It has a vegetable in it. Why can't we have breakfast cake?

Ellie takes a bottle of milk and says she can make hot chocolate with the chocolate bar and the milk. She rummages around and finds a saucepan and starts up the stove. Lys cuts up the bar into tiny pieces and add them into the warming milk. Ellie whisks it up with a fork and pours out four cups of frothy hot chocolate.

Right on time, Martha walks into the kitchen in some baggy brown pyjamas, her hair even more frizzy than yesterday!

"What's cooking, girls? I can smell something delicious!"

"We made you a hot chocolate! And would you like a grape on your cracker or peanut butter on your cracker?"

"Doesn't matter so long as it's crunchy. Ahh, it's nice to have guests!" she says with a smile.

GoGoal

Ellie

Lys and I are sitting on the pull-out sofa bed with Por Por's crochet blanket draped behind us keeping us company, poring over her letters to Martha. We're trying to fit all the pieces together like a puzzle. We try to remember Martha's letters. I'm so engrossed with the mystery of a life past. One that feels so far away but familiar. Then I find the one that makes my heart soar!

"Lys, Lys, you have to read this one," I say as I hand a worn, thin paper to her with care.

"This is it!"

Mei-Lan Lee
Flat 17, Block 9 Community Flats
1827 Orchard Terrace
Kowloon, Hong Kong

26 August 1969

Martha Goldsmith
9 Sandyview Street
Quiet Meadows, Australia

Dear Martha,

Confucius says we should feel sorrow but not sink under its oppression.

Today we did just that. It started six months ago. Little by little, I copied down in my own notebook all the names and addresses of the women who get paid $5 an hour.

My sisters and I went to visit all the women on the list. Many lived in the towns close to me and some a little further away and we had to take the bus. We took eight Sundays to get through the whole list.

I said this to everyone: "Hi, I'm Mei-Lan and I work at the garment factory. These are my sisters. You don't know me, but I know this. You get paid less than the male workers who do the same thing as you and I don't think that's fair. Why is what we do less than what men do? I don't want this to happen anymore because it's not fair to all the women who work in the factory now and all the women, maybe even my sisters, who might work there in the future. We must stop this. We stop this by stopping. We stop work together. We show them that unless we are treated equally, we won't work. We will strike and we will do this together."

Some were scared. Some wept. Some said no. Some laughed and said it was about time. Some got as mad as I did. Some were worried. I gave them all a date I had decided on – Monday 18 August 1969.

We met in the lunchroom when the factory opened. At first it was me and Toilet Button Lady (I found out who she was in the end) and her friend. Gradually two more women joined us. Then two more. Then three more. Eventually all 50 women I had spoken to sat together in the lunchroom and we didn't work. We sat there for three days, until Mr Davenport and Mr Mouse listened. After all, they couldn't keep making sales without us all working. They finally agreed that everyone would receive the same payment.

We won! We won!

Love, Mei

Lys squeals with delight. We do a dance from the bed and clink our mugs of hot chocolate together. We start talking all at once.

"I can't believe she did that!"

"She's so cool. I am so proud. And she's my grandmother! My Por Por!"

"Why don't we – "

"Totally, we can go and ask people to help – "

"Lucy tried to get money but it didn't work."

" – wow, we should do the same thing!"

"How, how? We can't strike."

"We need lots of people, rally up the people – "

"Where can we get lots of people?"

"FunStar!!! How many followers do you have?"

"Only 270 – it's like all the kids in my year, some other kids from school, the girls from our old soccer team and then randoms on top of that. But Ruby, she has over 500!"

"And Josie?"

"Yeah, she has even more. She goes to this dance school and knows people through that."

"Well, the three of you already have well over 1,000 and each of the people you know also have more… you see it's possible!"

"And we need to sell something. Not just randomly ask for money. No one just gives you money."

"The birdhouses… I was thinking about them yesterday… it's a bit like what Martha's done for us, giving us shelter when we're not home. Helping people."

"We need to be like Por Por. How she helped Toilet Button Lady. Talking to people, doing something."

"How? We still need money to make things. No one's going to give us money. We're just going in circles. Like these crazy flower circles on this crazy flower blanket!"

I watch as Lys traces the circles with her fingers going round and round. It's given her an idea – she jumps up.

"No, no, we're not going in circles. Ellie, you're the best! I know how we can raise some money!" Lys stands up and walks to the study, "Martha, can I please use your computer?" she calls out.

When I get to the study to see what she's up to, Lys is already frantically tapping away at a giant computer. She's got another idea and she's on a roll. I have no idea why I'm the best since I don't think I gave her an idea. I see her type in "GoGoal" in the search engine. I watch her amazed, wondering what the heck GoGoal is.

I peer over her shoulder to see where she's landed. A website where people post up their projects and ask other people to support them by giving them money to get their ideas off the ground.

"The blanket! I got the idea from the blanket when you mentioned the flowers. The knitting club used this website to sell their blankets and to raise money for their friend. We're going to sell our own birdhouses!"

Take flight

Lucy

"Come on, girls, let's take you home! I know a short cut. Lys, your mum will meet us halfway," says Martha as she bundles us all to the front door. She grabs her denim jacket and a set of humungous goggles that look like an oversized snorkelling mask from the hat rack. The jacket has big patches on the elbows and a big aeroplane picture across the back.

Everyone is quiet in the car thinking their own thinking. When no one is talking I feel awkward. I wiggle in my spot and decide it's a good time for riddles. Riddles are always fun in a car!

"Ah… er – what five letter word becomes smaller when you add two letters?" I ask.

"Ugh! Lucyyyy. Seriously," Ellie says.

"Wait. I've got this one," says Lys. "Short becomes shorter!"

"I've got one," says Martha. "I do not have wings but I can fly. I can go straight up and down. I can go sideways or forward or backward. I can land almost anywhere. I am a…" says Martha as she turns into the flight school. We are all staring out the windows at the little planes.

Everyone shushes up again. I think it's not just me now. Everyone is feeling awkward.

"Come on, girls. Get a wiggle on." We scramble out of the car and follow Martha to a small plane. She walks under the wing and disappears. We stop and wait.

"Double quick," she calls and we jog after her. She's heading for a helicopter.

We all look at each other and say at the same time, "A helicopter!"

Martha helps us all buckle in. She sits in the front as she talks to herself.

"Ok, pre-flight checks – done." We watch on. It's super awesome.

"Start engine – tick." The fan blade thingies start spinning. It's so noisy, I cover my ears. Martha shows us how to put on these headsets to protect our ears. Ah, much better.

Martha picks up a walkie talkie.

"Martha's Mover requesting clearance."

"All clear, Martha's Mover. Have a good day," the voice on the other side crackles back, and with that we're off.

We are hovering a little distance above the ground. We start to slowly move forward, getting higher as we go. It jolts and bumps and swooshes. We all scream and hold on to our seatbelts. My tummy turns. It's like being on those roller-coaster rides they have at the Easter show. All bumpy and jumpy. We all scream as the helicopter drops again. Martha laughs but doesn't turn around. She is too busy concentrating on all the buttons and dials. I've decided Martha's 120 – can you still fly a helicopter when you're that old?

The helicopter comes to a complete standstill in the air. Like magic. I can still hear the blades muffled through the headsets but we're not moving forward or backwards, just staying still.

Martha turns around and yells, "Is everyone okay?" She does a thumbs-up sign.

We all nod shakily and before we can say anything, she smiles and turns back around and pulls hard the lever next to her. The helicopter takes a super quick turn and swoops up over the mountains and we are off.

"Woo hoo!" I hear Martha cheer. I think she's crazier than me!

Aurum's house

TREE BRANCH!
CONTAINERS: 2 INSIDE, 1 ON TOP
FINISHING TOUCHES...
TA-DAA!
JUST ADD WATER!
DONE! A HOME FOR THE BIRDS!
WATER
SOMETHING TO STAND ON
FOOD
SHELTER
NESTING MATERIALS
AURUM'S HOUSE

Big sis, little sis

Lucy

I'm pretty loud. I don't have an inside voice. When I need to know something, I need to know straightaway. When I want to do something, I want to do it straightaway. I don't think about where my popcorn falls. If I love popcorn, I will eat it all the time for every meal if I can. I don't mind if other people don't like popcorn as long as I can still eat it. Yep, I'm ready for a rest. Popcorn is the perfect snack food. I'll eat some now. I go and grab a packet of popcorn and sit down.

I watch Ellie and Lys continue to work together on Aurum's house. It's a much better version than the one I first made from the book. They talk together about the prototype-thingy. About what material would last longer outside and they look up where to get different materials. They decide people will have trays at home they can re-use so no need to provide that. They agree on where they can get the instructions printed and that they want to use recycled paper. They ask each other what they think and they listen to each other's ideas. It actually looks hard to organise and plan and discuss.

Ellie and Lys giggle at something silly Ellie says. Ellie is the artist and draws everything up. Lys knows how things work. She is the builder and makes it real. Together they work on the idea. Ellie draws up the plan and Lys types it up on her laptop.

I sit quietly eating my popcorn and watch them tidy everything up. I usually like to run the show but not this time. Lucy is number one helper today! I grab a piece of paper and pencils from my pocket.

Lucy's rules...

#20   A little idea can become a big one

#21   Keep trying

#22   Somtimes you need your friends and your
        sisses help

#23   Always have pokets

#24   Chillax

Stepping up

Ellie

Well, I look at it this way – I can continue to stand in the water and let the waves crash into me – in the crash zone. Or I can just start swimming. With Lys by my side encouraging me, I choose to start swimming. Even if it's only a dog paddle.

I swivel around in my desk chair to face my laptop. I'm like an empress, cool, calm and confident. I decide I'm going to tell Mr Staples. Last year he was really supportive and encouraged me to enter the art competition. He'll know what to do, I trust him. Also, if this person was in art class with me, he needs to know.

I open up FunStar and go straight to all the @ellie copycat accounts. Deep breath. Lys gives me a gentle nod and my eyes well up a little. I'm so grateful to have a friend like her. I start taking screenshots, making sure I get all the videos and all the comments. It takes quite a while but I have them all. I attach them to an email and send it to Mr Staples asking for help.

Ding.

My heart sinks and Lys gives me a hug.

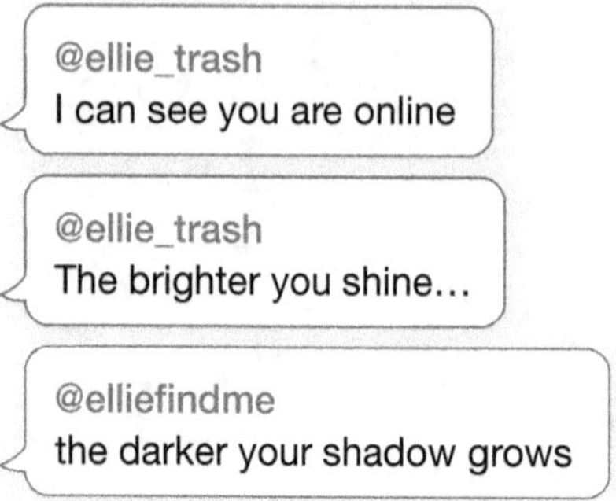

"Creepy," I say, as I screenshot these messages too.

"So weird. This bully definitely has some serious issues," says Lys.

"It's a bit odd that I still don't know who the bully is but they know me. What if I'm in class with them this year and don't even know it? Eww," I shudder.

Next I open up my account. 277 followers. Who are all these people? They all know about me but I don't actually know who they all are. I start going through them one by one. Flagging which ones are friends (the ones I know well and trust) and others, the ones I don't really know (this shadow Ellie, people I'm not in contact with anymore or I don't know very well and the complete randoms). Opening my account settings, I go to privacy and flick share with "friends only". That leaves me with 43 true friends and the remaining 234 are fake friends.

With that sorted, I lean back on Lys's bed. "I can't believe the bully is sitting there waiting for me to go online. Why are they so mean? To go to so much effort to set up accounts and write all of those things?"

"Hmm, I wonder if they're just super unhappy, so they lash out," says Lys.

"A bit like what Daniel did?"

"Yeah, like it's really nothing to do with you. It's about their own pressure to be the best at soccer or get an art prize," says Lys.

"But it still doesn't make it okay," I respond.

"Yes, that's true. You know, your dancing's pretty good, Ellie. Maybe the bully was jealous," says Lys.

"So now you help me, Ellie. You know I avoid dancing at parties because I don't like people looking at me. I feel so shy! I love to dance when I'm alone in my room and of course with you, but

I hate the thought of being seen doing it! By people I don't know! This is why FunStar scares me so much. People looking at you. I admire you, Ellie, for FunStar and putting yourself out there."

My cheeks warm with Lys's words. I smile and hug her.

"You know, Lys, it's awful when people look at you and you're stuffing up, remember I used to even hate putting my hand up in class in case I got something wrong! But you know what, what if that's okay? People generally care about what they're doing and worry about how they look, just like you. But if you do it in time together, you're in a group doing the same silly awkward thing, it's fine! On FunStar, so long as we're in a group together and dancing in time to the music, you won't stand out. There's so much to look at!"

I turn on my playlist and grab Lys's hands. We dance randomly, totally silly for a while. A chicken dance, some over the top hand swaying, hips this way and that.

I show Lys what I call the Cabbage Patch move. I put my arms out and bring them back in, rotating them in a big circle like I'm mixing a giant pot while bopping back on the spot. So random and silly. Lys joins in and we giggle, moving around my bedroom mixing fake giant pots, adding in some head bops for good measure.

This is the most excited I've been about dancing for a while and it's even better with Lys. It feels good that I'm helping her enjoy dancing again.

We do some hip hop type moves. Lys grabs her phone to take a clip of me doing some moves she likes so she can practise later.

I show off a bit, popping and locking to a fast beat. Contracting and relaxing my muscles in my arms and legs as quickly as I can. Arms up, pop and lock, arms down, pop and lock. But then I lose my place and end up messing it up! I laugh at myself with all the uncoordinated pops.

I try to do a spin-down shuffle where I lean awkwardly backwards and plant one arm on the ground, trying to cross my legs in the air at the same time. My arm collapses under my weight. I land flat on my back. Ooof! Lys leaps over me and does a "ta-da" with spirit fingers!

We go to the laptop so I can show Lys some of my clips. Lys clicks on some pretty old ones and they're bloopers and mess-ups. We are cracking up laughing at some of my old mishaps when Lys takes over and slices some of the hip hop I just did from her phone with some bloopers from my old FunStar clips.

We include when I spilt the cookie dough all over the floor in Shake, Make and Bake, the time I slid straight into a door rather than through the door frame and when I threw my microphone up into the air and it landed on my head. Lys and I are in hysterics as we boomerang the microphone drop right at the end. Over and over it drops on my head as my face screws up in shock. We are laughing so much, we are crying. My sides ache and my face hurts.

And then I make a decision.

"Lys, let's upload this one."

"What? Are you sure? You don't look very polished in these at all. Sure, we just said it's okay to stuff up, but they're so different from all your other clips."

"Yeah, I'm sure. It's what I want to do right now."

And so I copy the clip over onto FunStar and add the caption: *I am no longer hiding. I have learnt to speak from the heart, follow my heart and do what I love.*

I hold Lys's hand and click "post".

Go team

Alyssa

Not getting into soccer last year meant I didn't have to rush around and get to all the practices. I guess that was a good thing, with Por Por passing away and Mum moving to Hong Kong as it would have been tricky to keep it all going. But deep down I really wanted to keep playing. I needed something to do to keep my mind distracted from worries about Por Por and Ellie.

It was weird that I didn't get into the team as I increased my training more than anyone else who tried out. I was so determined that much to Mum's disapproval, I even practised dribbling the ball down the hallway at home. On top of that, I ran laps around the park on weekends and even did squats as I brushed my teeth!

All of that doesn't seem important anymore.

I eventually agree with Ellie that she can give Daniel my number. Seeing her stand up to an unknown online bully today made me feel stronger about mine. She must have done it just as she left to go home because I see a message from him after dinner. Even though I said okay, I really didn't expect him to contact me so soon.

I hesitate before I click on his message. My hands shake a little. Even though Ellie showed me their earlier messages, I expect him to change his mind and behave how I remember him. Mean and nasty. I think he'll mock me and say he lied to Ellie about wanting my phone number, just to have another go at me. I feel like I can cry at anything these days, so when I click on the message, I scan his words quickly right to the end to see if there's a "Haha, fooled you, four-eyes. I'm actually glad you never made it on our team. A slow-poke sloth like you would've slowed us right down." I steel myself for the disappointment.

Wow, I can really be mean to myself, can't I? I shake those thoughts away. That's not Daniel, that's the little voice on my shoulder I need to be wary of. I take a deep breath.

> Daniel
> Hey Alyssa, it's Daniel. Sorry I crossed your name off the list. It's pretty crap of me. We just lost Nationals and the parents got to me. I fessed up to Coach. Told him my head just hurts with everything. You know what I mean?

After I finish reading, I'm not upset. Actually, I feel relieved to know the truth from him. It wasn't personal and as Ellie said, everyone's just really worried about themselves and how they look. Maybe soccer is like dancing. You want to kick all the goals, but sometimes you just trip on your own feet?

Although not the usual message I'd get from my friends when they're sorry about something, I can tell Daniel's trying. I laugh and shake my head. Not a single emoji. I will never get boys. What would Martha and Por Por do? Should I accept that he's willing to change?

I feel sorry for him, for the pressure he's been under and for feeling like he had to do things like belittle others to make himself feel better. I don't know how that feels exactly and it's weird to me that anyone can feel that way. But I sit with his message for a while to try to understand.

Soccer was so important to me last year. It was comforting to be with a team, but I have my own team with Ellie, Lucy and now Martha. Por Por also from afar, in her letters, and Mum and Dad.

I pick up my phone and text back:

> **Alyssa**
> Hey Daniel – thanks. If you want to kick a ball around some time, let me know.

Alyssa's journal

Today I'm grateful for...

- Ellie standing up to the bully, so proud of her.

- Giving FunStar a go and actually enjoying it, who would have thought?

- Finding a new friend – Martha.

- Talking to an old enemy turned friend (maybe?) – Daniel. So strange and unexpected.

- The pack of choc-heart ice creams Mum let me buy at the supermarket.

Quote of the day

"An obstacle is often a stepping stone."

Anonymous

Crash

Ellie

I add some finishing touches to our GoGoal site. Across the top of the page I place "HELP the birds of Blue Lake" in large dramatic font. I carefully select some pictures. I have a beautiful one of a lyrebird with its amazing ornate tail on full display and a perfect pair of king parrots perched high in a tree.

What a team, I think, as I admire our work. Lys for her brilliant GoGoal brainwave, Lucy for her composting obsession that led us to understand that the birds needed help. I'm happy to be feeling normal again.

"Urgent security vulnerability" warns my laptop with beeps, bells and chimes pulling me out of my moment of calm. There are boxes layering up all over the screen. I try to close them but they are popping up faster than I can close them down. My computer has gone haywire. I flip my laptop closed before it seriously self-destructs!

Oh my goodness. I call Lys. "I've killed our GoGoal site, it's acting really weird. Boxes popping up everywhere and it's beeping and buzzing. I don't know what to do!"

"Oh no! Hmm. Okay. Don't panic. I'll come over and help you. See you soon."

I'm pacing down the hallway when the doorbell rings. I swing it open. "LYS! And, oh hi – Daniel?"

I let them both in. Lys sees the strange look on my face, smiles and nods. She has a plan.

Daniel takes a look at the computer. "Virus attacks can be from people who put bots on the internet that carry viruses to hack into your website."

"Do you think it could be one of the bullies?" I ask, trying not to cry.

"Bullies? Oh, you mean online. Wow, that sucks Ellie. It could be anyone, to be honest. These bots are a bit like the insects of the internet. They crawl around the internet and if one gets attached to your website, others swarm and cause it to crash."

"Eww." I shudder, imagining insects crawling all through my computer causing it to malfunction. I hate creepy crawlies. Why would someone do this? Why take down a website that is trying to help birds? These people have some serious issues they need to sort out for themselves.

"Can we fix it?" I ask.

"I can try," says Daniel, opening my computer. He's clicking away, working quickly and methodically. He goes into settings and turns off pop-ups which immediately stops all the screens piling up on the computer. I have my fingers and toes crossed, and I'm pretty sure Lys does too.

"Okay," says Daniel, "now let's run the anti-virus software and fix this up.

"This might take some time. Hey, what were you working on anyway?" says Daniel, sitting back. Lys and I get Daniel up to speed. How the bushfires have been making the birds from Blue Lake travel for food, water and shelter. How Lucy designed a birdhouse but it was all cardboard, sticky tape and glue so it started falling to pieces. How it gave us an idea to do something better but how we now need money to start producing enough houses to help the birds.

We show him the designs and he nods, interested in what we have created. "This is pretty awesome. Hey, how about you do this part here? The branch might fit better this way? You could put it coming out the front if people don't want to drill or cut the wood. Also you could add fastening straps to help secure it onto a tree. I know where you can buy some of this stuff cheaply too. My mate Edo, his dad owns a hardware shop. I'm sure he'll help." We nod at each other, all good suggestions.

Daniel restarts the computer. Lucy is watching now, too. We hold our breath while it starts up. The screen goes black for what feels like forever. Up pops the login icon. We high five! We are back in action.

Divide and Conquer

Alyssa

This mess.

I stare at the pieces of paper and cardboard cut-outs, splinters of wood, scraps of rags and dried super glue bits lying about on our dining room table. Crumpled paper and chocolate wrappers are strewn on the table. There's a smear of chocolate on the floor. Oh yeah, that was me.

There's so much to do now that the website is up. I was playing around with the prototype birdhouse this morning. But now I throw myself onto the sofa. I don't know where to start. A cushion sticks uncomfortably into my back and I toss it onto the rug. Ellie has set five days to raise the money for the birdhouse kits and now time is ticking.

"Five days to get everything done," I think again. "That's not enough time. What do we even need? We don't have anything. We don't even know if we can get everything we need! It's too much work!" I stare at the messy dining table again. I better clean it up before Mum sees it.

My phone pings with a text message. Ellie's sent a photo of two king parrots standing on the saggy cardboard version of the birdhouse in her backyard. Even though the cardboard has totally drooped in the middle, the king parrots look cute.

The photo was what I need to get going. I'm a whirlwind of activity, tidying up the mess, throwing rubbish away. Once everything looks tidy, I sit down at the table and turn to a fresh page in my notebook.

I write a list of the items we need to sort out. If we split them up into tasks for each of us to work as teams, we might be able to get through it. I get out my laptop and draw up a table.

What	Where	Who
Wood pieces, fastening straps and glue	Hardware store	Daniel and his friend Edo
Cotton wool and towel pieces	?	Ask Ellie's Aunty Jam
Bird seeds	Pet store	Me and Ellie

Okay, that looks manageable.

That leaves Ellie and me with the bird seeds. I quickly look them up online and it's so confusing all the different types of seeds and prices. Some are as much as $10 a pack!

I look up pet shops and there are three nearby. I ring one and ask whether they have seeds for a wide variety of wild birds. The girl on the phone has no idea and says they have mixed bags of seeds at $7 a pack. The man at the second pet shop is knowledgeable and tells me a lot about bird seeds. He says they have tonnes of bird seed and that one with sunflower seeds is definitely the best. The third pet shop tells me they have sunflower seeds for $5 a pack.

I decide that Ellie and I should give the second pet shop a visit.

Alyssa
Me again, Ellie! Can you come with me to a pet shop to check out bird seeds? Like soon?!! And could your dad give us a lift there?

I think about eating seeds all day like a bird and how I wouldn't like that at all as I make a peanut butter sandwich for lunch. The bread is multi-grain. I pick out the seeds and eat them. They're okay but there's no flavour. Lucky I'm not a bird! Maybe birds don't have taste buds.

Daniel
Hi Lys, Edo's dad can help, no problem.

Alyssa
Great! Thanks, Daniel!

I go onto the GoGoal site and add a link in there to Edo's dad's hardware store to thank him for being on the team.

At the shops, Ellie's dad heads to the supermarket and gives us an hour to sort out the seeds.

Ellie stops me outside the pet shop.

"Hey Lys, I told Mum and Dad yesterday about the bully."

"Oh, I'm glad, Ellie. What did they say?" I reach for Ellie's hand and give it a squeeze.

"I don't know why but I was so worried they would be angry at me. They weren't. They said I did the right thing by reaching out to Mr Staples. They are going to call him when school's back next week and make a plan."

"Did they make you delete FunStar?"

"No, not in the end. We talked about it but they agreed it was better to keep watch and they'll help me. I feel much better now." Ellie smiles a little. "And this makes me feel better!" She points to three fluffy puppies in a small pen at the front of the store.

"Yap yap yap…" they bark, jumping up and down, their tails wagging.

"Ohhh, so cute. I want one!" squeals Ellie. She scoops down and picks one up. The puppy licks her face and she laughs.

A guy who works there walks past. His name badge says, "Hi, I'm Dave."

"Welcome to Pet Palace, are you looking for a puppy? These mini schnauzers sure like you!"

"Not a puppy, we're looking for birdseed," I say. "We're trying to make a birdhouse."

"Hey, you're the girl asking about the sunflower seeds earlier!" Dave remembers our conversation over the phone. "Yeah, you can't go wrong with sunflower seeds. They're over here, I'll show you."

Ellie reluctantly puts the puppy back down, scratches his tummy a few more times and follows Dave and me down an aisle of bird care accessories.

"Do you know if birds have taste buds?" I ask.

"Sure do, but less than us. A parrot has 300 to 400 taste buds, while humans have around 9,000. A bird that lives on nectar and fruit will like sweet tastes more though."

"What about king parrots? What do they like?"

"You can try giving them some banana as well as seeds."

Ellie shows Dave the GoGoal site from her phone and explains our plan to him.

"Fantastic! How about this? I can sell you a bulk pack of sunflower seed at cost. I'll put them into little compostable bags as starter kits, $3 a pack. If you don't mind, I'll put in an ad for my store and they can come back here and get more!"

Our eyes light up. A discount and a supporter! We thank him, spend a bit more time cuddling the puppies, then head back to meet Ellie's dad. With my head clearer now, I think we will get there one step at a time.

Adventure with Aunty Jam

Lucy

Aunty Jam loves the secondhand shop. She buys all her clothes there and always has the best outfits. Bright orange jeans with a matching tie-dye top. Cowboy boots and a denim jacket with tiny sparkles on it. When Aunty Jam was little, she never really got many new clothes. They were always pre-loved from her cousins or her mum's friends. They would patch up any holes and sew buttons back on. She says that too many people now buy lots of new clothes and then just throw them out when they're sick of them or a button drops off, which is why she still buys lots of her things from the secondhand shop. She says it's just like recycling your plastic bottles and containers.

And I love going into the secondhand shop with Aunty Jam. We play a game where we pick up an item and tell a story about where it's from. Like the time we found a golden necklace that had an Egyptian picture and hieroglyphic writing on it. I imagined that the necklace was from the Lost City and was worn by the king of the city. One day pirates plundered the city stealing all the treasures they could find. This necklace was stolen by a pirate called Stinky Jenny and her parrot Buster. She wore the necklace every day for five years, three months and two days until a terrible battle at sea occurred between two pirate ships. Unfortunately, Stinky Jenny lost the battle and her necklace fell to the bottom of the ocean.

The necklace was washed around by the tides over the years. Fish and dolphins attracted by its sparkle would pick it up and play with it. Eventually it was carried into Australian waters, where it was washed ashore on a small beach. One day a man collecting seashells picked it up. He donated it to this secondhand shop, not realising what a treasure he had found. And that's where Aunty Jam and I, with our eagle eyes for hidden treasures, found it!

So when Ellie says it's my job to go to the secondhand shop to get rags for the birdhouse, I jump with joy. Aunty Jam and I have this covered.

"Aunty Jam, over here." I run over to the corner of the shop that has big baskets labelled "last chance bargains".

"Perfect, and look it's only $1.50," says Aunty Jam as she pulls out an old holey jumper and puts it in one of our reusable shopping bags.

"Lucy, we only want natural fabrics – wool or cotton. No polyester or plasticy fabric," says Aunty Jam, double-checking the label of the jumper.

"Only the best for the birds and their babies," I say, tipping over one of the baskets so all the clothes spread out on the floor. There's an old white t-shirt with marks, denim jeans with big rips, a brown woollen scarf (obviously not a popular colour this year), cotton pants with a drawstring without pockets (no wonder they made it to the secondhand shop – not practical).

We go through all the bargain bins and check the shelves, too. We have five shopping bags stuffed full of clothes. Aunty Jam carries three up to the counter and I follow, dragging the remaining two across the floor.

The man at the counter chats away as he folds the clothes and writes down all our items and prices on a piece of paper. I tell him about how we are making birdhouses. He is so impressed he asks me to make a sign so he can put it in his window to encourage people to buy one.

"There," he says, "that will be $62."

Aunty Jam and I look at each other, and I know we are thinking the same thing.

"Bargain!"

Not winning a race

Alyssa

The sun shines through my window and wakes me up. I had a dream last night where I was in a race. Everyone was a different animal. We had to swim across a great river and the first twelve animals to get to the other side would be the winners. I remember the start of the race, lining up with a rabbit, cat and dog. There was a whistle and we all jumped into the river. All the other animals swam ahead of me. After a little while, instead of swimming, I swooped up and flew among the clouds. Maybe I was thinking about one of Martha's letters where she described her flying, or maybe I was a dragon, soaring high above the world. Maybe I was thinking about my trip to Hong Kong.

In the dream I was having fun. I didn't worry too much about the race. I zoomed about, up and down, round and round, flying with ease and looking down on the little towns below, enjoying the scenery and taking my time. I don't remember what happened next or whether there was more to the dream. It's funny about dreams – you remember the feeling and bits of it, but never the whole thing.

This dream feels familiar. It's like one of the stories in my old storybook of fables. I get out of bed and go to my bookshelf, searching through all the books until I find the fables book, *The Great Race*. In the story, the Jade Emperor organises the race to decide the twelve animals of the Chinese zodiac years. There's a picture of the dragon, majestic and brilliant, strong and kind. Even though the dragon has the speed and strength to fly ahead and win the race, it stops midway to help a village by bringing water to the villagers, then it sees a rabbit struggling on a log in the river and with its breath, pushes the rabbit onto shore to win fourth place. The Jade Emperor praises the dragon for its kind nature and awards it fifth place.

When Por Por and I used to read this story together, we would stop at the page with the dragon and marvel at the drawing with its green scales and purple torso. The illustrator had made the dragon's skin shine like armour with broad strong wings. But the eyes are drawn round and clear, like it can see everything. Sometimes Por Por would tell me other dragon stories.

I close the book and put it in my backpack. I want to give it to Lucy to read. She's into dragons lately and I know she'll love the story since it has so many animals in it.

I realise since coming back from Hong Kong and helping Ellie with the birds, that finally things are falling into place. I'm taking the time to do things that I love with my friends and help others. I snap my backpack shut. Sure, the dragon's a clear strong winner and it could have rushed to the finish-line, but it doesn't seek that out. It's just fine coming fifth, having saved a village and helped a rabbit along the way. That's why dragons are awesome.

Follow me

Ellie

I'm lying on my bed scrolling through my FunStar feed when I stop on one of my favourite accounts @skippit. This girl is an awesome contemporary dancer. I love watching her stuff but this time it's something different – she's at an animal rescue shelter. She's talking about all the animals that need homes. There's Luna, a grey cat who's 12 and was found hungry on the street with bald patches on her body. Sally and Frank, brother and sister Jack Russell puppies, who were abandoned on the vet's doorstep are looking for an owner with lots of energy. Skippit girl's encouraging people to adopt dogs and cats that desperately need a home.

My mind drifts to GoGoal. The site is up and running but now we need to raise money. It costs $20 to make the birdhouse. With a goal of 150 birdhouses, we hope to raise $3,000. That's so much money. That is more money than my entire lifetime of pocket money, birthday presents and Christmas money put together if I had never spent any of it.

So far, we have a grand total of $250. I check again. Still the same. The donations are coming in slowly, very slowly. Mainly from our family – our parents and Aunty Jam, of course. But no one else is clicking on our site. I look at the post we did on FunStar to promote the page. It has the website details and a brief description about the birds and the birdhouse.

I glance back at the rescue animals. I have an idea! We need our FunStar post to be more fun, get the point across better, more like this adopt a rescue animal one. I have less followers these days but if we all post the clip – Josie, Ruby and me. Even with Daniel's @DanielSoccer account, that's more than 1,500 people. That's got to help. This is going to be a team effort.

I think of a simple routine, jot down some notes and grab a bunch of props. I call Lys to talk through the plan and we get to it.

I grab my satchel bag and start heading to the park. I text everyone I know to meet me there.

Ellie
Lys and I would like to invite you to a group FunStar video to help save the birds at Blue Lake. Meet us at Lovells Park at midday. Wear something bright and be ready to dance!

Ruby
I'm in – luv this!

Josie
Me too. Can't wait x

Daniel
Thx Ellie. Bringing some mates if ok

Aunty Jam
Count me and Gerald in! I'll drag him away from his gardening.

Mum
Ellie can you clean your room first?

Ellie
Mum, get off the group chat!

I head to the park. Lys's mum drops her off to meet me there an hour early to set up and sort through the plan. Lys drags out a large suitcase from the boot of their car and shows me all the things she's brought along that might be useful.

Lys has her bright jumper with the strawberries on. It looks fab. I laugh when I see it and she does a little twirl. It's perfect.

We run through the dance and make some changes to keep it simple for everyone.

Aunty Jam arrives with her neighbour Gerald, who's brought a guitar! Gerald is also a carpenter and he's offered to help cut all the wood into the right sizes for the birdhouses once we can afford to buy it. I give Gerald a high five.

They've also got some lunch and a picnic blanket.

We find a sunny spot in front of a large beautiful gum tree, as our friends start arriving. I set up the tripod with my phone and make sure it has the right angle to get everyone in. Aunty Jam and Lucy hang up lanterns onto the lower branches and make garlands with flowers Aunty Jam has brought from her garden.

A kookaburra comes by and sits on the branch, curious at what we're doing there. Lys take some photos so we can include it in our clip later.

Daniel arrives with Edo and a couple of his friends from soccer. I vaguely recognise them – how quickly we've changed. Maybe they think I look different from our soccer days, too. They've brought some soccer balls and are practising tricks. We agree to add some tricks in the moves since the boys are keen to show them off.

We teach everyone the simple routine and Gerald plays his guitar. Mum and Dad are so embarrassing because they want to do the chicken dance, but I think it will look fun. There are a few added suggestions and we take it all in. After a couple of run throughs, we're ready to tape.

Together we sing and dance, flapping our arms as wings, shaking an imaginary tail and clapping our hands while we count. We are ridiculously good!

Josie and Ruby finish up with amazing jazz cheer moves with cartwheels and backflips. Then the soccer team does their tricks. Everything falls into place.

Everyone takes their time to pack up. The day is beautiful and soft. Lucy and Aunty Jam lie on the grass and chat some more, while Lys and her mum sit under the tree with some snacks. Mum and Dad are still dancing with Gerald playing on the guitar and I think how awesome sometimes things can be.

I'm keen to get the clip done and loaded up, so Lys and I say goodbye to the others and walk back to my place.

We spend the next couple of hours engrossed in editing the clip, adding extra music, voice over and subtitles.

"The 94 bird species in the Meadows Peak and Blue Lake region rely on the diverse variety of vegetation types to sustain them for food and as their homes," I read out.

Lys takes over. "Help us to help them by buying a birdhouse which we designed to shelter the birds in your own backyard. Go to our GoGoal site by clicking here. Building your very own birdhouse will give our native birds a home."

Viral

Alyssa

$250… $320… $1,800… $2,560… $3,220…

The ticker keeps going up and up and it's not stopping!

Ellie, Lucy and I stand in front of Ellie's laptop watching the sales come in. It's incredible. The amount that's going into the GoGoal account has been increasing ever since Ellie posted the clip on her FunStar account. Gradually at first, and then at a quicker pace.

Everyone in the dance shared it, and we asked Martha to put it on Meadows Peak Aviation's social media. They sent it to the birdwatching research team who put it on their birdwatching group social page and tagged in the local council who then put it on their website. After a while, we couldn't follow where the clip went.

We reach our target and then some more. We don't know what to do with the extra money because we only have so many birdhouse kits, and so we call Martha for some advice.

"Hi, Martha! Can you hear us? You're on mute – the microphone thingy, press that!" We gesture exaggeratedly at the computer where we know her unmute button would be. We put our hands to our ears and mime that we can't hear her. Finally, she gets it.

"Oh yes… now can you hear me?" yells Matha, and we nod back. "Great, girls. Hello! How are you? Loving this video call thingamajiggy. I don't even have to get out of bed! Hang on, just grabbing a cuppa." Martha walks off into the distance.

"She's still in her pyjama bottoms," Lucy giggles.

"But with a nice top! She should just stay in the whole thing!" Ellie points out.

"Again, what's the point of pyjamas?" adds Lucy.

"I'm back. What did I miss?"

"Martha, we have some good news. Thanks to you and all our friends and family, we've done so well! We've more than hit our target but now we don't know what to do," Ellie explains.

"That's a good problem to have. How much extra?"

"We only have 150 kits so we really only need $3,000. Now we're around $3,720 but we can't get more wood and rags quickly enough. That's all we have," I explain.

"How about you write a message on your page and thank everyone for their support. You can say the kits are all sold out – make that nice and bold – and offer to send other people their kits in a few weeks' time. People won't mind. The other thing you can do is tell people if they would prefer, you could send them the instructions on how to make the kits themselves by sourcing their own materials. That way, their extra donation can benefit the birds of Blue Lake even more."

"That's a great idea!" Ellie says.

"I thought this might happen. So I have some good news. I've already spoken with the Board of the Meadows Peak Aviation Foundation and they are happy to help you take the donated money and make sure it goes to benefit the birds. It will go towards our conservation program and we'll set up a program to support the local birds.

"I'm proud of you, girls. Your determination and spirit… ahhh, it makes me think of me and Mei. If only we had one of these video contraptions in our day! We could have saved a lot of money in airmail stamps. They were expensive – and we only did a long distance call on our birthdays. It was tough on a teacher's salary."

Shipping

Ellie

BEEP, beep, beeppp, BEEP beeppp!

"That will be Aunty Jam!" I say. Lys and I race each other down the hall. Aunty Jam is parked in front of our house and is busy pulling the trestle tables from the back of her car.

She passes one to Lys and one to me, and we awkwardly crab-walk them inside, down the long hall and into the backyard. Aunty Jam is right behind us carrying another table in one hand and balancing a big plate of freshly made lamingtons in the other. She puts the lamingtons down on the small side table against the fence with the other food before straightening up and stretching out her back.

"This is positively chaos, girls!" laughs Aunty Jam, looking around.

Mum and Dad have made a stack of sausage sandwiches and Lucy has made five gigantic jugs of lemonade. Lucy is so excited she has been up since 5am squeezing lemons. I smile and wave at Lucy, she grins back.

Lys and I get busy setting up the trestle tables. We have a plan to make this into an orderly productive chaos! We line the tables up creating three stations. It's just like an assembly line in a manufacturing factory. Each station is responsible for one task and then passes their portion to the next station. Por Por would have been proud of us.

Everyone has turned up today to help and our little backyard is packed. Edo's dad is lining up the hardware supplies with Edo and Max's help. Lucy is busy pouring lemonade for everyone. Martha and Aunty Jam are taste-testing the lamingtons. They are so caring towards us, like we're their lost birds!

Daniel has printed all of the address labels for us which he lines up on the last table. Ruby and Josie set up the speakers. They pop on a playlist they have created which apparently has every song they could find about birds and flying. Lys and I survey the situation, our eyes sparkling.

There is a cheerful babble of conversation in our little backyard. *I'm Like a Bird* hums through the speakers.

Lys nods at me and with that I cup my hands together, take a deep breath and whistle loudly. "FWEET! Okay, listen up everyone! Lys, Lucy and I are so happy you are here. Thank you for your help! Today is going to get a bit crazy. We have 300 birdhouses to ship."

"Whoot, whoop, yipee," everyone chimes in.

"Yes – that's a lot. We need to work as a team and we need to be organised, so here's the plan," I say.

Lys jumps in. "This is station one. Edo and Max, you're with me on this one. We are responsible for putting all the materials together. You need to put in five pieces of wood, a handful of nest materials, glue, a bag of bird seeds, fastening straps and the instructions. It's all written down here." Lys points to the instructions on the table. "Over to you, Lucy."

"This is the boxing station. You need to stuff and squeeze all of the things into the box like a present. Josie, Ruby and I are here." Lucy is smiling from ear to ear.

"Thanks, Lucy. And station three is our quality check. Daniel and I will take care of this one. We will check the box is in order, that things are neatly stuffed into the box," I smile at Lucy. "We'll tape it shut and pop the labels on."

"Dad and I are going to stack them in the ute to take to the post office," Edo cuts in.

"We'll keep you chickens hydrated and fed," says Aunty Jam. Martha gives a thumbs-up, her mouth full of lamington. With that, our production line is humming.

Upgrade

Lucy

Standing a little taller today, I hold in my arms my very own birdhouse. This one is solid and is an awesome home for a beautiful bird.

I've spent all morning painting this birdhouse. Putting splotches of light green and dark green and brown paint. Blending the colours together so it will be camouflaged in the tree. Glueing sticks and dry leaves to the side. It has taken forever to dry. Exactly three and a half episodes of *Yunlong and the Dragon Traders*. Finally, I touch it and my fingers do not stick and get covered in paint. Okey dokey! It's ready!

First things first. I need to remove my saggy and crumpled birdhouse from outside. My cardboard birdhouse is looking miserable. It's blown out of the tree three times in the wind this week which has resulted in spilt water containers and soggy cardboard. Time to go – I pop all the old pieces of the birdhouse into the recycling bin. As Aunty Jam would say, "Reduce, reuse, recycle".

So here I am standing in front of the tree with my birdhouse. I couldn't have done it without my big sis or Lys or Aunty Jam.

With strong arms I place the house in the tree and wiggle it around so it sits all snug. I secure it in place with the fastening straps, pulling them tight so it won't move. Next up is the water and bird seeds. I run inside with the containers and fill them up until they are overflowing.

Balancing the water container in one hand and the container full of sunflower seeds in the other, I head back outside.

I'm concentrating really hard and staring at my hands and the containers so as not to spill too much on the carpet as I go.

Gold flashes from somewhere in front of me. A spark of light. I look up, and there sitting in my bird home, is Aurum. She looks magnificent. Shimmering in all shades of gold.

"Cluck cluck," she says.

"Aurum! I made this home for you and all the birds that need help," I say.

"Chirp," she says, as if to say yes.

"I hope this birdhouse helps you and your friends, Aurum. I've been so worried about all the birds."

"Chick," Aurum is listening carefully to me.

"You know sometimes I pick fights with my sister, I know I shouldn't but…"

"Cluck cluck."

I bury my hand in my pockets. "It's just Ellie is always getting attention, she has all the nice things. Sometimes I just wish I could be the cool one, just once. Just like Ellie."

"Chirrup chop," Aurum understands me.

"You're right, it's a bit silly. If it wasn't for Ellie and Lys, we never would have made all these birdhouses and then what would have happened. It could have been terrible."

"Chick."

"I hope you love your house, thanks for listening, Aurum," I feel lighter, having said all of that.

"Chip chop," says Aurum, flapping her magnificent wings. She flies off, leaving glitter trailing behind her and a single golden feather. I put the magical feather into my pocket.

Launch party

Alyssa

The road towards Meadows Peak Aviation seems so much shorter from a car.

Mum and I are driving down Lorikeet Road. I smile. Was it only a week and a bit ago that Ellie, Lucy and I took that train trip to Meadows Peak? So much has happened since that day. We made new friends, we overcame bullies, we helped the birds find homes.

I look out the window and nod hello to all our soldier friends with their ribbon dresses. I'm glad the bushfires are easing and that things are getting better for them.

We come to the end of the road and there is the centre. It doesn't look so scary now, no padlocks on the gates and the front door is open and welcoming. We climb the stairs and peer inside.

Martha's back is turned to us. She's setting up some food and drinks on a table pushed to the side of the open seating area. She hears us approach and she turns, a wide smile across her face, grinning ear to ear. She rushes over to give Mum a huge bear hug and then another one for me. Her eyes are glassy as she gives Mum another hug and pat on her head

"Sorry, love, I forget you're in your forties now!" she says to Mum, with a wink to me.

"It's so amazing with the latest technology I can now keep in touch with you better than I've been able to in the past. All that letter writing I used to do. Do kids write these days?" she asks.

Mum laughs and chats with Martha about this and that, until Ellie, Lucy and their parents arrive. They wanted to catch the train again to show their parents the awful platform.

Ellie and Lucy talk at once.

"… then there was a family waiting in front of us…"

"No, Dad wouldn't let me get the burrito chips again. They were soooo good!"

"Mum saw that awful old station. She said there was a tourist attraction there a long time ago but they closed it."

"I told her about the scary kidnapper cat! How funny was that?"

"Okay, only funny now, not then. Sure, it was scary."

"So scary!"

"And your sandwich, Lucy…"

"I was actually really hungry afterwards but I didn't tell you."

"You were so brave!"

"Okay, girls, enough noise. Wow, what is this rabble? This is why I never had kids," Martha explained to the adults in an aside.

"We can hear that!" we laugh.

But we finally calm down. The snacks look tasty and I pass a cookie to Lucy and take another one for me. We sit down on little poufs which are usually laid out for their clients waiting for scenic flights.

A couple of people who work there come in and one of them gives Martha a thumbs-up. Martha looks at her watch and clears her throat.

"I have a little something I want to say and share. As you all know I love to fly – always have and will. It's in my blood.

"I wanted to fly all my life, ever since I was a little girl. In those days it was hard to learn to fly for a woman. So I thought I could start by being an air stewardess! But that was a disaster – just not the serving tea type, I don't think."

"This iced tea is nice," Lucy says.

"Thanks, sweetheart. It wasn't until after I became a teacher and was a bit older that I saw this little place here and they were looking for someone to teach local history to the staff who work with the tourists. Instead of paying me, I asked Barry who owns this place to teach me how to fly. I love it here and the people have been so kind. One thing I've learnt is that you will get to where you want to be somehow, even if it's in a curly wurly way.

"Mei and I were such good friends in high school. We didn't always keep in touch. In the eighties I was quite bad actually, travelling a lot and figuring things out.

"I love seeing your friendships and that you have each other's backs. I love that you know you live in a bigger world and love the animals and the world around us. On that note, I want you to come outside with me."

We follow her outside to the runway. Ellie and I glance at each other and shrug. We have no idea what she's up to. I look at Mum and she shakes her head, curious as well.

When we're outside in the sun, it's warm and lovely. The smoke has gone now and the air is clear.

There's a loud whoosh up above and we glance up. A plane flies above. Loop de loop, it swerves. Behind it I see white smoke coming out of its exhaust, as words start to form in the air.

We whoop and cheer as the final letters form in the air. And then a heart! Ellie takes hold of my hand and I give it a little squeeze. In front of us, Lucy stands still looking in awe at the sky. Her head is tilted back, her eyes are wide and for once she's quiet. Normally when she's excited she goes nuts, jumping up and down. But not this time.

Ellie's eyes dart towards her then back to me catching my eye. I shrug with a little knowing smile. I feel there might be a pilot obsession coming up.

"Ellie, where's your phone?" I ask.

"Oh here, in my pocket," Ellie says, taking it out. "Good idea!" she says even before I say anything.

Ellie reaches her arm out with her phone, as we swivel around to get the words behind us. Gently, I nudge Lucy for her to turn around and Ellie quickly takes a selfie of us. She sends it to the group chat from the viral dance day.

This is our tribe.

Ellie + Lucy + Lys

Alyssa's journal

Today I'm grateful for...

- Ellie, Lucy, Martha, Aunty Jam, Ruby, Josie, Daniel, Edo and Max.

- Lucy's crazy idea to save the birds of Blue Lake.

- The three pieces of cake and four handfuls of raspberry smashes I ate at the party today.

Quote of the day

"Anything is possible when you have the right people there to support you."

Misty Copeland

It's a wrap

Ellie

I sit cross-legged on my bedroom floor, fanning out my inspiration cards in front of me.

"I love these cards," Lys says, sinking into my plushy beanbag. She looks through my cards with the confident Empress and the cool Dragon. "Can you draw me another one? I think we need an Architect. You know how much I enjoy creating something. Thinking about how to make something work and putting it all together."

"Yep, I like that!" I start to draw Lys an architect, with her pen, notebook and calculator, figuring things out. "And what about when Lucy followed us all the way to the train station?" I ask.

"I think she is an Adventurer, just like Martha's tarot reading in Paris! Lucy had a vision that the birdhouses could help the birds to survive the bushfires. She really goes for it when it's something she believes in," Lys says, writing Adventurer on another card.

"Let's add one for Aurum, the Songbird. Her strength is to listen and to really understand you. It's like she can really see you," I say.

"There are so many positive people out there like Martha and Aunty Jam but sometimes you forget because of the bully. Should there be a card to remind us of this?" Lys asks.

"I don't want to remember! But you're right," I agree.

"And even though there are those horrible bullies, there are also supportive people like your art teacher who can help you out," Lys adds.

"Hmm… how about we leave that as the Shadow, then? It's a good reminder that we can say mean things to ourselves. Our shadow self. Or we don't like what others think or say about us. We need to try to not let it become too overwhelming," I say.

"You sure stood up to your shadow with the bullies, Ellie. We actually ended up having so much fun together that day when we made the blooper Funstar video to get back at the bullies," says Lys. "Oh, there's something I want to show you."

Lys takes out the battered moon cake tin from her backpack. "I added another letter to the tin. This is my letter to Por Por."

Dear Por Por,

You used to tell me the story of the Jade Emperor who said to the dragon, "Why didn't you win the race when you can fly?" I never understood that. I always want to win, come first in a test at school and kick the ball into the goal. I finally understand what it means to be a dragon.

You used to give me the juicy lychees and eat the sour ones yourself.

You loved colour. You said moving away from your family was a very hard thing to do. You made yummy pineapple tarts.

You once told me about your friend Goldie who taught you "cuppa", "dang it" and "gotta go to the loo." You said Ellie reminded you of her.
I agree.

You used to knit beautiful jumpers and blankets for everyone you love. You once made me a pink jumper, with red strawberries all over it. I never thanked you properly for that. I love it.
Thank you.

Love, Alyssa

"Por Por would treasure this letter," I say, giving her a hug. I rummage through my satchel bag. I pull out the selfie we took at our launch party. The one of Lys, Lucy and me.

Smiling, I lay the selfie out with all the cards we have created in front of us.

To all the brave girls in the world, here are our cards for inspiration. Borrow their strengths to help you through those tricky times and sticky situations – they'll give you a little confidence boost when you need it most.

We're lucky to have each other. We are a Tribe.

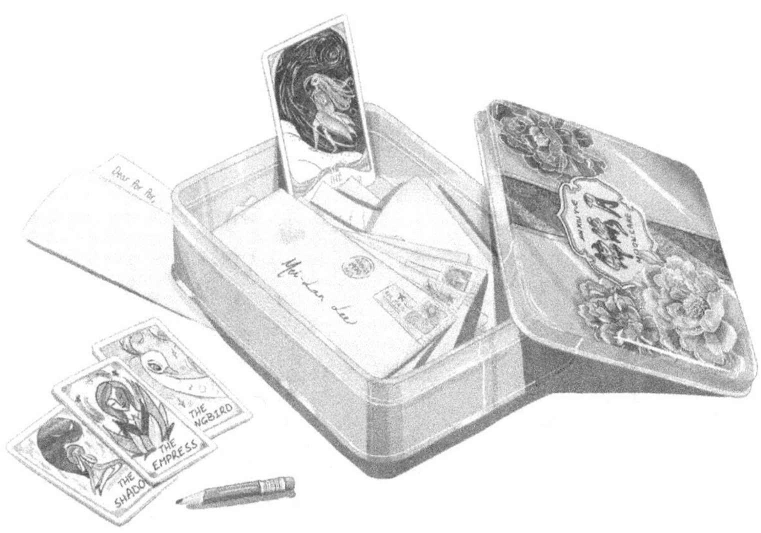

The Empress

I am confident
in myself, I am
balanced and I am
enough. The Empress
is at peace with
herself and her
surroundings. I do
not need to share
every personal
detail with my entire
social network.

The Songbird

My strength is in the
art of listening. I can
truly listen beneath
the surface,
understand and sing
back what I hear
others say. The
Songbird or Ayrebird
is a mythical
Australian bird.

The Tribe

I have friends
and I can be
myself. I choose
friends who are my
cheerleaders and
support me. Life
is more fun with
friends. The Tribe
helps me find my way
through this world.

The Dragon

I am the Dragon.
I breathe out
clouds. These clouds
produce rain and
renew life. The
Dragon is not afraid
of pressing reset
and starting again.

The Architect

I understand how
things work. I am
curious and focused.
The Architect is
a builder and a
planner, using their
logical thinking to
achieve their goals.

The Nurterer

I am warm and kind-
hearted. I like to
cooperate and think
about other people's
feelings. I deserve
to be treated
with kindness.
The Nurturer is both
soft and strong.

The Adventurer

I like to explore
and try things out.
I enjoy connecting
with others.
The Adventurer
follows their heart
and does things
they love.

The Shadow

The shadow is the
voice in your head
that tells you
that you can't do
something. It is also
the mean comments
people say that
upset you. Is your
shadow self holding
you back?

The singing firefighter

The hot air came first. Then came the smell. Burning smells replaced the soft freshness of the eucalyptus leaves. The air was thick and heavy. Then the sky turned black.

Lottie shook her head. She flapped her wings around her face to move the smoke away.

What was that orange flickering over the gully? To Lottie, it looked like the people's cooking light. When the people came to stay overnight in the floppy caves, they would take fallen branches and make an orangey glow over which they waved their food. Sometimes the food came from round shiny holes, other times they popped soft white fluffy balls on sticks into the flames. They really liked the white food, Lottie guessed, since the littlest people would squeal with delight when the balls turned gooey and they licked their funny fingers.

Sometimes careless people left the shiny holes lying around. Lottie didn't like that. Once she found a bit of the gooey food on the ground and pecked at it. It was awful! She had clicked her beak and rubbed her face up and down over some bark to get rid of the sickly stickiness.

Lottie loved her home. She was a lyrebird. Lyrebirds don't fly, so she lived in a hollow of large tree roots by herself. She loved to sing and copy noises. She would copy the rumbling sounds of the big metal boxes the people travelled in. Usually she would sing first thing in the morning, but not that day.

That day with the hot dry air, Lottie was getting restless. She decided to look for Waldo, her neighbour. Waldo was a wombat. He lived with his family in a burrow near the creek. She wanted to ask him why the sun had turned red, why the sky was black and why she was so thirsty. Normally she would drink once for breakfast but today, she was really thirsty.

Lottie found her neighbour moving leaves around. "Hey Waldo," she cooed, "what's going on?"

"It's gonna get bad real soon. The red storm is coming," Waldo said. "The bushland is burning. Look over there. We need to get ready."

Lottie followed Waldo's gaze. She saw a lot more of the flames, dancing their way closer. She had not seen a storm like this before. Purple lightning was shooting from the sky near the gully. It was so hot.

"The orange flames?" Lottie asked. "I've seen the people's food go brown and melt because of them. Sticks crumble into nothing, leaving grey flakes on the ground. Will that happen to the bush?"

"I've seen this happen before. Not the whole bush, but lots of it. You're not safe in your leafy hollow. Follow me."

Waldo led Lottie to where his family was. Nestled in the burrow home was Nelly and their three young ones. It looked pretty snug already.

"My family's been making burrows around here over the years. Over there by those tree roots, you'll find an entrance, another one by the creek and there are lots more. I scratched marks near the entrances. Like this." Waldo showed a marking which Lottie made sure she remembered.

Lottie left Waldo and went to the creek for water. To her surprise she saw a bunch of other lyrebirds there. She nodded to a few she recognised. Everyone looked scared.

It was getting hotter and Lottie started to worry about the flames getting too close. After she finished drinking, she looked at her long feet and claws, useful for digging out wriggly bugs for lunch. Once when the people's fires were left smouldering, Lottie used her feet to clear up the mess, shuffling the leaves away. That gave her an idea.

"We need to do the same thing," Lottie thought. She gathered the lyrebirds and showed them how to bury the leaves so there was nothing for the hot flames to burn. Lottie and Joie went west of the creek, Jack and Morty to the eastern side. More followed and together they quickly formed a clearing around the creekbed. The lyrebirds felt safer and set off to look for burrows nearby.

Gradually they found shelters for everyone. It was just Lottie left. Some of Waldo's tunnels were well hidden, but birds have pretty good eyes. Lottie heard a crackling noise from behind. Her heart beat faster. She turned as Jack rushed to flap her out of the way as a ball of flames the size of a boulder jumped the creek!

Jack nudged Lottie under a big piece of bark and with it balanced on his head, pushed her towards a small opening in the ground. She didn't see Waldo's markings. But Jack urged her forward. "Squeeze in, Lottie. You can do it!"

Lottie wriggled so her feathers could flatten. With her feet, she raked and raked to widen the opening. Jack did too, still trying to balance the bark on his head. The air felt hotter and Lottie's throat was thick with smoke. Finally, Lottie's feet slipped into the hole, with Jack's weight behind her they tumbled in together. They were safe!

Lottie could feel it was much cooler in there. She was still in shock when suddenly Joie was beside her, flapping away the dust from her face and hugging her.

Lottie felt grateful for her friends. Together in the wombat burrow they waited a long time. The time it would take the sun to go from the edge of the land to the middle of the sky.

Eventually, they emerged. First peeking their elegant heads out of the burrow. Once they were sure it was safe, they walked towards the creek. Everything was different. Everything was black. The trees were bare. Trails of smoke billowed from scorched earth. Lottie saw a lizard family lying still on the ground. They were too late.

But like a haven, the creek had not been touched. The raked ground stood as the birds had left it. Shoots of green grass stood standing in the mud.

Jack, Joie and Lottie looked up and saw all the lyrebirds standing around the creek. Shocked but safe, Lottie started to sing. The others joined in. A mixture of their own song and a melody of all the birds and noises of the Australian bushland.

Find us at thebeingbravegirls.com and follow us
@thebeingbravegirls

www.ingramcontent.com/pod-product-compliance
Lightning Source LLC
Chambersburg PA
CBHW071155180726
48291CB00007B/2470